BRIGHT

A BRIGHT SUNSET

OR

Recollections of the Last Days of a Young Football Player

BY

J. H. WILSON

This editon © copyright 2006
Christian Focus Publications
ISBN: 1-84550-114-4

Published by
Christian Focus Publications Ltd.
Geanies House, Fearn, Tain, Ross-shire,
IV20 1TW, Scotland, Great Britain.
www.christianfocus.com
email: info@christianfocus.com

Cover Illustration by Jean Baptiste Camille Corot
Cover Design and inside illustrations by
Dannie van Stratten

Printed and Bound in Denmark
by Nørhaven Paperback A/S

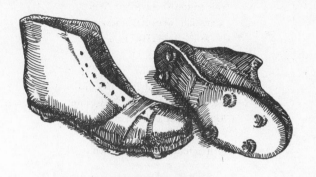

With thanks to
Mr George Thomson
for his recommendation
of this classic Christian testimony

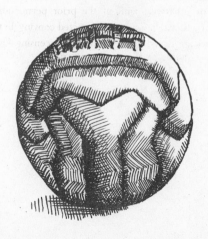

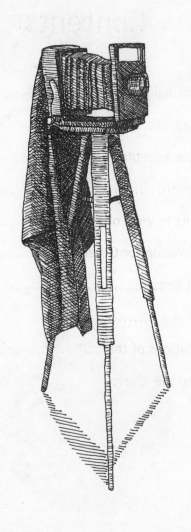

Contents

The following papers were never intended to meet the public eye. They were written by a mother to her only sister in America, with all the unreserve with which one loving and sorrowing sister writes to another. As the letter was being read over, before being despatched, her husband expressed the desire to have a copy for their own use. The copy thus made was seen by a few friends interested in the young sufferer and his bereaved parents; and in deference to their opinion that it might be useful to others, the narrative — which, with the exception of one or two sentences, is simply a private letter — is now published.

It seems to be specially useful to the many young men and boys who are so enthusiastically devoted to what may now be said to be a national game. The publication of the details of the last days of a young and ardent football player, is not meant to damp the ardour of football players. Fatal accidents on the field are happily very rare, and the experience recorded in this little book may not be often repeated. But this account of one of their number, bearing up so bravely and patiently, in the midst of severe suffering, looking calmly and hopefully on the approach of death, and, at length, by simple faith in Christ, passing joyfully into the Lord's presence, cannot fail to interest, instruct and stimulate other young men. It is vitally important that the spirit manifested by this young sufferer should animate the robust and energetic youth of our country and time, and that, while earnest in business as in sport, they should also be 'fervent in spirit, serving the Lord.' One cannot look on a young life so brimful of energy and enthusiasm, without longing to see it consecrated to the service of Christ and the world's highest good.

EDINBURGH J. H. W.
October, 1884

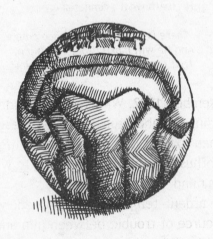

The Football Accident

'No chance has brought this ill to me;
'Tis God's sweet will, so let it be,
He seeth what I cannot see.

'There is a need—be for each pain,
And He will make it one day plain,
That earthly loss is heavenly gain.'

In November, 1882, William Easton Riddell was attending Bellahouston Academy, Glasgow. He was then sixteen years of age, full of life, eager and enthusiastic about everything to which he set his mind.

His ardent temperament, indeed, was the only source of trouble between him and those about him. When interested in anything he was apt to become forgetful of everything else. His food, his sleep, his health, all were forgotten for the time. This disposition to get engrossed in the thing he had in hand at the moment, was sometimes a cause of anxiety and trouble. When he found an interesting book, for example, he would seek a quiet corner, where he thought he would be sure to have no interruption, and then throw himself on the floor and read on for hours, quite oblivious of all that was going on in the house. Skating, football, cricket, he enjoyed intensely. Boating he went into with great ardour. Part of each summer was spent at Toward (in Argyllshire), and there he always seemed to attain to the height of earthly happiness. His uncle David had boats of various sorts, and his kindness and sympathy with him as well as his great liking for the sea, went far to make Toward the earthly paradise which it was to Willie.

One day in the beginning of November, 1882, I remember well my young son's arrival from school at four o'clock. After his usual very hearty, affectionate greeting, he said brightly, 'Oh, mother,' he said to me, 'do you know your son was nearly killed today?'

'How was that?'

'Well, sit down beside me, and I'll tell you. When I was playing at football...'

'Oh, well,' I interrupted, 'you must not come home

and tell me anything that happens to you at football. You know how I dislike that game. I wish you would give it up.'

'Well, but mother, wait till I tell you how it happened. There was a scramble over the ball in the playground. I fell, and hit my knee on a loose round stone, and a lot of fellows tumbled pell-mell on the top of me — and oh, the pain! I really thought I was killed — killed at football at last, as you have so often prophesied about me! Oh, it was dreadful, Mother! If you had only seen me go hopping around!'

I did not say much. He took my face between his hands, and looked right into my eyes with so much fun, saying 'Mother, be sorry for me! I like to see you look vexed about your nearly-killed boy! You're not looking vexed!'

At that moment a companion passed the window, and just saying hurriedly, 'Oh, there's so-and-so; I want to speak to him,' Willie bounded out of the room, and we saw him run round the side of the house as lightly and nimbly as ever. We who were left so abruptly could not but be amused at the sudden termination to his sad tale, and I said, 'Doesn't he look like a killed boy!'

How little we dreamt that he had then really got his death-blow! There was no mark left by the accident, but the end of one of the thigh bones had been hurt. Once or twice during the winter he spoke of having growing pains, and I remember him saying, 'I had no idea growing pains were such sore things.' He walked such distances and scampered about so much, and with such delight, that we never gave these remarks a further thought.

In the following April, about the end of the month, when standing talking with some companions after a game of cricket, he accidentally struck with a wicket stump which he had in his hand the same spot which had been hurt at his football six months before. The pain was very sharp for a minute or two, and after that he always limped a little.

In the beginning of March the four youngest children had been sent to Toward for a little change. At the end of a fortnight we noticed that Ettie, the youngest still at school, seemed to be pining for the other little ones, and her father took her for two days to Toward. On the next day after going there she was decidedly ill, and could not be brought home. It turned out to be measles, and I went down to nurse her. One after another the five little ones were laid down. In the two youngest, congestion of the lungs followed, and we had almost ceased to look for their recovery. Sophie, three years of age, seemed to be sinking, and a message was sent to Glasgow for the others to come, that we might be all together when she left us. They were all gathered round her bed one afternoon, a tearful, sorrowing group, to take the last look and give the little hand a last kiss. We did not expect her to live above a few minutes; but she was mercifully spared and given back to us, and proved a great joy and comfort to dear Willie in the last part of his journey.

As soon as we saw there was hope of Sophie's restoration, the children all returned to school in Glasgow, that the house might be kept quiet. On the 26th of May, dear Willie was again sent to Toward – this time that he might be cared for by his mother, as his knee was paining him a good deal.

I could scarcely detect any swelling about the knee, but Willie felt sure there was. We got the doctor, and he thought there must be inflammation at the knee joint, and advised rest. At first he was confined to the sofa, but he was continually forgetting to keep the knee still, and would be here and there before he remembered. Then he would make to keep his bed. It continued to swell gradually, and the doctor decided to put it in a starch bandage.

We left Toward on the 28th of June. Willie walked up the long pier at Wemyss Bay. We drove from Paisley, and he was allowed to sit outside the cab. His father helped him up, but at our door he jumped down quite smartly, and took my hand to help me out. When I found fault with him for not waiting to be assisted, he said so cheerily, 'Oh Mother, I didn't jump on my sore leg; I just hopped down on my well one!' He dragged me off at once to see his brood of white chickens before I got off my bonnet; and from his light, happy way that day, it was impossible to think his knee could be very bad.

Willie had become very much attached to the doctor, and taking this into account, along with the fear of having a change of treatment for such a very important part as the knee, we asked him to come up to Hillington and bandage it. He did so, and said Willie must lie still for a month. Just as the bandaging was finished, the dear boy grew very distressed, and almost fainted. It had to be undone and bandaged a second time.

We saw it still distressed him, but he was anxious to bear it if it was the right thing. His father left the house with the doctor, and soon after, Willie almost fainted again. When he recovered, it was to burst into hysterical tears. I proposed to take the bandage off, but he said 'Oh no; perhaps this strange feeling will wear off.' I soothed him and cheered him to the best of my ability, and by-and-by he fell asleep. Gradually he seemed to get accustomed to the pressure, and for a while we awaited the result. After the first two days, Willie was wonderfully happy. Everybody was kind and thoughtful about him, lending him books and coming to see him.

His father left on the 30th June to visit the congregations in the Presbytery of Dingwall, as a deputy from the General Assembly. There seemed to be no good reason for breaking off this engagement.

A young friend of ours called with a beautiful bouquet of flowers; and knowing that he was to lie for a month, she proposed to send a water bed which she had, and which she thought he would find easier than an ordinary bed. She was leaving next day for the Continent, and so sent it at once, lest, by any chance, we might decide to use it. We were not long in finding out that this was a very special token of our Father God's care. We scarcely realized what a comfort it was to Willie, till one day he was obliged to do without it.

His room became a favourite resort for all the household. Little Sophie scarcely ever left it, and as baby was only five weeks old, she had to be much beside her mother. His room was thus a very bright and cheery place. He seemed to enjoy this new kind of life exceedingly.

I remember saying once, when I brought his little tray with his dinner to him, and he had welcomed it in a happy, sprightly way, 'It's not often that invalids are so glad to see their dinner.'

'Oh, Mother, you must remember that your coming with my tray, and fixing me up in this style, is one of the pleasantest varieties in my day just now!'

'Yes, Willie, but I think your appetite is very good also – better even than when you were going about.'

His health was really so good that I felt him rather a trying patient.

When I was putting his knee right one day, he was so full of fun and frolic that I said, 'Willie, I feel you quite a tax on my patience; I wish you could be quiet and let me get on more smartly with my work.'

He just gave me a kiss in a petting way, and said, 'Oh yes, mother, I know I am an awful tax on you; and I have just come to the conclusion that when I get well I must 'study for the ministry,' as they say, and try to repay you for all this. I know you would like to see your eldest son a minister! Of course I would be a minister of the old school, always arguing, contradicting, finding fault, but after all, having the Church's real interests at heart. Now, mother, dear, you needn't turn your head away; I see you're laughing. It's quite true. I am serious. I do not see any other way of paying my debt to you, and you'll forget all this when you see your son in a pulpit, Dr. William Riddell, and read his speeches in the papers!'

I had read to him the General Assembly news in May, when he was suffering from inflammation of the eyes. I feared that he was reading too much in bed, and consulted the doctor. He thought two hours' reading in the forenoon and two in the afternoon were quite enough. This was a great deprivation to Willie, but he said to the doctor, 'Oh, well, I'll try and be content with that, if Mother will talk or read to me the rest of the time.'

He questioned me about all sorts of things insisted upon my putting in words my reasons to my opinions on such things as novel-reading, theatre-going, and dancing.

One of these days, when I had not sat much beside him, I brought him something and was leaving the room again, when he said, with a sigh full of mirth, 'Oh, Mother, that you were not so much of the swallow tribe! I do wish you were more of the nightingale! — that you would sit beside your son more, and let him hear your sweet voice oftener and longer. You alight here and give one or two chirps, and then you take your flight to some more summery clime, where there's a wee baby or something of that kind, and I am left out here in the cold. I hear you going 'flitting about from tree to tree,' and always expect that you are going to alight beside me, when off you are again. Do come just now, mother; I have a hundred things at least I want to talk to you about!'

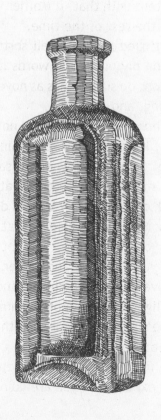

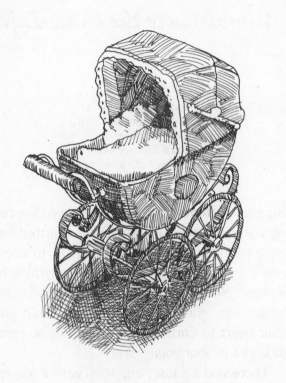

Glimpses into the Inner Life

'He who of our inmost hearts
Every hidden thought divineth,
And His people from their sins,
Like a precious ore refineth,
Give us grace that we may say,
"Darkness now hath passed away,
And the true light shineth."'

His grandmamma came out to see him. She felt very sorry to see such an active, spirited boy lying bound to his bed, and to help to cheer him she gave him a pound to get anything he wanted. Whilst she and I were sitting sewing beside him, she said, 'Willie, you should give your heart to Christ; it's a nice thing to come to Christ in your young days.'

There was a pause, and then with a roguish smile he said, 'Gran'ma, what leads you to think that I have not done that? Mother, what is there in me that makes gran'ma think that way?'

I answered, 'Willie, facts will stand, thinks will not. See you to yourself in this matter.'

I remember his saying one of these days: 'Mother, Father really must let me try for the 'Welfare of Youth' prizes. I could do it lying here.' And another time: 'The first time you are in town, you might call at the Religious Institute Rooms, and get information for me about the Civil Service. There's no saying what this leg of mine is going to turn to, and I am as well to be preparing my head to be useful.'

I felt sure that Willie had constant and sore pain in his knee at this time, but no one could have gathered that from his behaviour. He never grumbled about his leg, and never looked discontented.

He began to be very careful to have his books always left at night within reach. I asked the reason; he answered: 'Because I sometimes wake very early in the morning, and I weary, when I cannot go to sleep again.'

I felt a little uneasy on hearing this, for Willie had always slept soundly till morning.

Next morning I came quietly to his room about four, and found him wide awake, his great blue eyes looking away out across the country. He did not know of my presence for a moment, and I had time to have the anxiety I had felt the night before greatly increased, and the thought at once arose, 'I must try to lead that dear boy to have more direct dealings with the Great Physician.' When he turned and saw me, the look of joyous surprise was touching.

It was a lovely bright morning; the sun was streaming into his room and I said:

'My dear boy, why are you not sleeping? Is your leg very painful?'

'No; but when I waken, I cannot go to sleep again.'

'Oh, but you must go to sleep again, that's all that's about it.'

I lay down and took him in my arms. After a few words of prayer, I sang the 'Happy Land,' and then lay quiet. In a little he felt sleep stealing over, and roused himself to say:

'Oh, what if we should both fall asleep, and dear wee baby alone up in your room?'

'Well, I intend to sleep, and I intend that you should sleep too. If baby does wake up, I'll hear her first cry.'

'Would you? How is that? How do you hear so quickly?'

'Well, dear, I think that verse helps us to know about it, "His ear

25

is ever open to their cry." I feel that my ear is very open to my baby's cry. God made the mother's heart and the mother's ear. And "He who made the ear, shall He not hear?" Doesn't this help us to know that The Lord's ear must be very open to His children's cry? Think often about this, Willie, when you are left alone and in pain.'

He asked and answered some questions on the subject and I saw, in his thoughtful, expressive eye, that he had taken in a new and brighter idea of prayer, and of the readiness to hear and answer that must be in our Father's heart. We slept, and in two hours he awoke thankful and refreshed, and said, 'Oh, what a delightful sleep I've had! Did you sleep? Has baby never wakened?'

From this day I have reason to believe he prayed about everything temporal and spiritual.

Through his illness he often referred to 'that morning, Mother;' and I can never be sufficiently thankful that I was led to come down and have that talk with him before he became so ill.

How often after this, and so soon after, was he made to feel that for him there was no help of man at all! Those who watched by him, and would willingly have borne his pain, had to go to rest when fairly worn out: he had to suffer on; and hence his unfailing refuge was the One who never left him, and whose ear was ever open to his cry.

On Friday, July 6th, I noticed Willie a little more thoughtful and quiet than usual; and once when I was sitting trying to make out, over the book in my hand, what might be in his mind, our eyes met. I had not counted upon this, and I was quite conscious that I was looking very anxious. Not willing that he should know how anxious I was, I said quickly, in a light way, 'A penny for your thoughts, Willie dear.'

'Mother, that is just what I was wanting to say to you; do tell me what you were thinking? I'll give you two pennies for yours just now!'

I turned off the subject by saying, 'Ah, mine are worth far more than that.'

He laughed at this, and we said no more.

Next day, I was sitting at the window sewing; I felt certain, without looking up, that Willie was not reading, but looking at me. I had begun to feel anxious and uneasy about his leg, and was feeling at the moment very much inclined to break down. I thought of leaving the room, but just then Willie said, in a calm, calculating sort of way, 'Mother, do you know that my leg is very VERY sore?'

'Is it, dear?'

'Very sore, Mother!'

'Do you think it is sorer than it was?'

'I scarcely know. I think it must be, for it's really very sore.'

The first time I could leave him, I sent off a note to the doctor asking him to come on Monday. He had not intended to visit on the following week unless sent for.

On Sabbath the eighth, very unexpectedly he said, 'Mother, I can't bear this; I believe the bandage is hurting my leg.'

'Well, your leg is not intended to be sore in the bandage, the doctor said so. I'll take it off.'

'Well, I think you should.'

I proceeded to do this.

He said, 'it may be very difficult work. Perhaps the doctor will be vexed at us for meddling it?'

I went on, however, and found the limb marked as if it had been too tightly bandaged. It had been gradually enlarging under the bandage. I wrapped the knee in cotton and bound the leg between two soft pillows, and he felt much easier. I then thought I should like Professor Macleod to see it, and arranged with the doctor that he should meet Professor Macleod here for consultation.

Wednesday, the 11th of July, at 4 pm, was the time agreed upon. It was my dear husband's birthday! An hour before they came, I was arranging some lovely flowers that had just been sent, when the thought suddenly crossed my mind, 'What a shock we would get, if Professor Macleod should think Willie's knee very serious, and might even speak of amputation! I knew Willie was in no way prepared for this; so I sought an opportunity at once of saying to him, 'Do you know what I have been thinking about my boy and his leg? 'Better to enter into the kingdom of God lame, than having two legs to miss it!' Maybe my impulsive, headstrong, wilful Willie was going to run too fast with this world, and forget about the Better Land, and this is to be a check!' There was no response. 'What do you think Willie; isn't it better to get lame into heaven?'

'Oh, yes; but there's no need to be lame to get there!'

The doctors arrived at the time appointed. I was present at the examination. Willie did not seem in the very least put out. I saw him look at Dr. Macleod admiringly, not at all inquisitively or anxiously. It was evident that Professor Macleod did not take many minutes to make up his mind what it was, and that it was very serious. The doctors then retired to another room. While I waited to be called in to hear his opinion, Willie kept me from feeling it such a trying time, by his remarks on Professor Macleod.

'What a nice looking man he is! What a pleasant, agreeable manner! It is a very nice face! Nobody could be afraid even to get their legs taken off by a man like that! He knows how to finger a sore thing,' etc., etc.

When asked to join them in the drawing room, I felt I already knew as much as I could well bear. I did not like the thought, however, that this sorrow had been caused by an accident, and in hopes that Professor Macleod would say it arose from the delicacy of his constitution,

I asked that one question. In answer, he said,
— 'There is not doubt whatever about that, the
hurt at the football is the cause. The second
blow has irritated the part still further.'

I could not go into Willie's room for some
hours. I gave baby in charge to Agnes, and
asked John and Catherine to stay beside Willie
for a while. I did not think it right to let them
know anything at all then, till I had had time
to think. Some hours after, when I did go in
to Willie, he put out his hand and said, half
jestingly, —

'Really, mother, would you be so vexed if
your teasy, troublesome boy were taken from
you?'

He did not ask anything, and never spoke of
Professor Macleod's opinion, and I felt relieved
and thankful. Next day I asked the doctor in
attendance to tell me frankly all he knew
about Willie's leg. He declined to do so. At last
I said: 'You must tell me this one thing at least:
Is this to cost Willie his leg or his life?' After a
little hesitation, he said, 'The latter.'

'Then,' I said, 'will you tell me what it is
that makes you so sure of that, when there is
so little to be seen?' After assuring him that I
could then and there hear anything he had to
tell me (I felt inwardly 'all that Thou sendest

me, my Father, Thou wilt give me strength to bear'), he unwillingly said, — 'Well, it's cancer, cancer in the thigh-bone, and amputation is of no use!'

'How long is it likely to take to run its course?'

'Well, a year; some are longer and some shorter, but the average is a year.'

Oh, what a terrible blow! Our darling, precious Willie dying, and dying of cancer! Every day of the year to follow, seemed in an instant to pass before my eyes! I was so busy examining these imaginary days, that I forgot everything around, until the doctor's voice aroused me, saying, 'Now, I told you that you shouldn't have asked me! I knew you couldn't stand it.'

For a few hours after he left, I kept away from Willie's room. I could not shed a tear. To get directions how to help dear Willie down the Dark Valley, was my one concern. Before I ventured to see that dear, bright face again, I wrote praying friends, asking them to help me. I had resolved that he should not be told it was cancer, as the information could only alarm and not help. I thought it better to prepare his mind gradually for what seemed to be in store for him, without startling him by telling him that he must die; and instead of turning his eye in upon himself, by any direct question about his spiritual state, I thought it would be better to lead him on to an easy and natural expression of his mind, in the course of our familiar conversations.

In the evening his brother John and I were left alone with him. They were talking cheerily and happily together. I felt it an awful thing to sit by, listening to their bright, light-hearted talk, with such a terrible secret in my heart.

I knew that Willie had almost perfect confidence in his mother, and could not possibly suspect that I was hiding anything from him.

The boys noticed that I was dull, and did not seem to be interesting myself in their conversation. At last they asked me something, and I said, 'Well, boys, do you know there's nothing I can think about tonight but a verse in the second psalm. It has quite taken possession of me. Try and guess it.

Willie said, 'Well, Mother, we give it up; tell us.'

'It's that one, "Kiss ye the Son, lest He be angry." I let them think for a little; then Willie said, 'Mother, we have submitted ourselves to Christ, and given our allegiance to Him – that is what is meant by kissing the Son.' (His father had preached a sermon from that verse some months before.)

'My dear boy, don't you feel the depth of mercy there is in that word 'lest'? It tells us He is not angry with us.'

'No.'

'Even this leg of yours cannot have been sent in anger?'

'Oh, no.'

'It cannot have been permitted heedlessly?'

'No.'

'We know God is too thoughtful about His children for that. Then, Willie, He must have a purpose in it. Isn't it really a pleasant thought to you that God is taking an interest in you specially, and training you as one of His children? It's a great honour, Willie, if you can only look rightly at it.'

He looked down at his leg, and smiled in a questioning way.

'What if this had been sent on you in wrath? How difficult it would be to bear this trial, if we knew we were at enmity with God!'

'Oh, yes, Mother; that would make a great difference.'

This answer, and the spirit of loving confidence shown in the manner in which it was spoken, gave me unspeakable relief and comfort. I asked John then to leave us and go to bed. When he had gone, I said, 'Now, Willie, will you try to remember, all through this illness, whatever pain you may have to bear, that it is a hand of love and care that is laid on you — the hand that was nailed to the Cross for us? Keep looking to Him, and He'll help you to bear. I am anxious that you should have this fixed and settled in your mind, for I believe the human body is capable of very intense suffering.'

I saw him about to say something, and fearing he might ask some questions which I did not wish to answer then, I said hurriedly, 'I hope God may not see this necessary for you; but we will try and leave it entirely to Him, and we'll look to Him to carry us safely through. Satan watches for a pained, distressed body, that he may slip in an unkind thought of Jesus; so you will be on the watch. Remember, dear Willie, that nothing would make this leg such a trial to your father and me, as so see you rebelling and fretting under it.'

He seemed a little surprised at my continuing to speak so earnestly, and asked, with evident sorrow, 'Do you think I'm very impatient and fretful?'

'Oh, no; we do not think that at all; but the doctors think it a very bad knee, and if they don't get the disease checked, it might get very much worse, and you remember the warning, "Watch and pray, lest ye enter into temptation." You might be hurried into temptation by your pain, and I want you to be prepared.'

He answered, 'Oh, I don't think I would ever have any feeling of that kind.'

The Issue Accepted

*'There is more of sorrow, but more of joy,
Less glittering ore, but less alloy;
There is more of pain, but more of balm,
And less of pleasure, but more of calm;
Many a hope all spent and dead,
But higher and brighter hopes instead.'*

Two or three times in the course of his illness, when suffering greatly, we asked if there were any rebellious thoughts; and the quick, astonished look and tone of rebuke as he answered, 'Oh, no!' were very reassuring. Once, when overcome by pain, he burst into tears. Recovering himself, he said, 'Do you think He'll be displeased with me for this? It is very sore, — very difficult to bear.'

'No, darling; He knows our frame, He remembers what we are; knows well what you are suffering at this moment. We are glad to see you get relief in tears, although it is trying to us; and do you think He is less pitiful? He would only be grieved if He saw you unwilling to take this suffering at His hand, or questioning His right to lay it on you.'

'I don't feel in that way, but I would not like to do anything to displease Him; and I can scarcely keep from crying, it's so sore!'

It struck us as being very remarkable that, after times like this, there should never be a look or expression of peevishness or fretfulness. He seemed always to calm down into a state of perfect peace and rest of mind and heart.

'Thy children shall be all taught of God, and great shall be the peace of thy children,' was being so literally fulfilled in his experience, that our feeble faith was scarcely able to take it in.

After prayer with him, I left him for the night. It was a great trial to me to leave him alone, knowing what I did know; but I thought it was better to make no change that night.

On Friday the 13th, John and I moved Willie into the drawing-room. We placed his bed across the large oriel window, and he was delighted with this arrangement, the view from his pillow was so varied and extensive. At first he was a little doubtful about taking possession of the drawing-room, and wondered if his father would not object. His father came home about midnight. He had not intended coming home till next day, the telegram about Willie's state not having reached him. But a strange, unaccountable uneasiness about us all, made him arrange about that evening's service and come home.

Next forenoon his father went to town to consult with the doctors, and I felt I must try and speak plainly to Willie. When tidying his room, as usual, I began by speaking of the way God carries out His great plans and purposes for us; mentioned one or two things interesting to Willie, where we should have done differently; and at length said, 'Wouldn't it be strange, Willie, if this lame leg of yours should land you in heaven? It may be part of His plan that you should get to see Him first of us all: before dear Papa, who has been studying and preaching all these years about Him; and before dear Gran'ma, or Gran'ma Carslaw, who have been reading and learning about Him, and waiting so long to be taken in there.' I couldn't say another word, I was trembling; and although I would have given anything to see his face, I dared not look up from dusting the crumbs from the carpet. If Willie had said, 'What do you mean, Mother? Am I dying? or, Am I not to get better?' I am sure I should have fainted.

The moment's pause before he answered seemed to me a long time. In a pleasant, easy, meditative tone, he said, 'Yes, it would be strange; I think Grandmamma Carslaw would think it wasn't very fair!'

In this quiet response I could not but recognise the answer to our prayers, that he might be prepared for what was before him; and yet I was surprised. His quiet, composed answer filled my heart with deep gratitude to God, and I felt able to sit down and have a talk with him about the home above. I remember that he was interested and pleased with the thought that it was a place that suited the inhabitants in every particular way. I finished by saying, 'What a bright and glorious place to be promoted to in such a hurry! I think I'll feel thankful to know that you have got there with one bound.'

I was very much overcome then, partly through reaction from the severe strain I had been under, when beginning the conversation; and Willie looked up so pleasantly, took my handkerchief, and wiped away my tears very softly, saying, 'I don't think you look very thankful, or very happy either, at the thought of my getting all these fine things before you.'

It was proposed by friends that we should get a certain specialist to see dear Willie. We should not have taken this step had the doctors who were attending him entertained any hope of his recovery under their treatment; but as they told us frankly they had none, we thought it best to ask his advice. Willie heard us talk about this and when we were alone on Monday, the 16th, he said, 'Mother, why do you want this specialist to come to see me?'

'Your doctors can do no more for you, Willie. God, of course, can make you well, and we are still asking Him to do so. He might send the answer through this man.'

'Do you think that I'll get better?'

'Well, dear, I cannot say. It seems to me that there is One praying on the other side, "Father, I will that they also whom Thou hast given Me be with Me where I am; that they may behold My glory which Thou hast given Me."'

'That is what I think, Mother.'

That was the first direct question about the probable issue of his trouble, and the first time he had been plainly told that his doctors could do nothing for him.

41

On Wednesday, the 18th, the specialist saw him. He was a little more hopeful than the other doctors, but he did not hide from us that the case was a very serious one. He prayed with us, and his gentle Christian spirit and manner soothed and comforted both us and our dear sufferer.

The doctor who attended him when at the coast, visited him towards the end of the week. He still held the opinion pretty decidedly that amputation might save Willie's life. Our knowledge that we owed little Sophie's life to his skill and attention, made us unwilling to relinquish the faint hope thus presented. In the perplexity arising from the conflict of opinion, our thoughts turned to Professor Simpson, who had been our medical adviser before he went to Edinburgh, and on whose interest and skill we felt we could rely with the most perfect confidence. I said, in Willie's hearing, 'How I wish I could see Professor Simpson and get his advice!'

He said, 'No, no, you must not get any more doctors for me;' and added with a smile, 'try the faith cure!'

On Monday, 23rd, father went to Edinburgh to explain Willie's case to Professor Simpson, and to ask whether he would advise amputation.

Professor Simpson kindly offered to come through and examine for himself before giving an opinion.

We felt this to be another special token of our heavenly Father's loving-kindness. In no other way could we have got such a feeling of rest and satisfaction as this gave us.

We had arranged that Uncle David should come on the afternoon of that day to baptize our little baby. It was a very solemn and touching service. We felt that we were presenting not one but two to the Lord, although we expected Him to receive them in two different ways. Willie joined in the service very heartily, and enjoyed it very much. He stretched out his hands at the close of it, that he might get little Edith May and give her the first kiss.

Professor Simpson came on the following afternoon. Just before his arrival, Willie said, 'Mother, I wish to see Professor Simpson alone. Do you think you can manage this for me? If you can, please do it. I want it very much.'

Professor Simpson told us that there could be no doubt as to its being cancer. His father then said, 'Well, doctor, there is just one question we want to ask: If he were your boy, would you amputate?'

'No, I would not,' and gave as a reason, that he believed the seeds of trouble had been carried to the lungs. He parted from us with the words, 'You'll find the everlasting arms very tender.' We learnt afterwards that he wrote of his visit to us, to his sister: 'It is a fiery furnace the three are passing through — father, mother, and son — but the Fourth is with them.' This was an exact description of our circumstances in a very few words.

When the doctor left, it was with fear and trembling I went up to his room. As I entered, he turned his head to me with a calm, pleasant smile, stretched out his hand to me, saying, 'Come away, my dear mother,' and patted and kissed my hand fondly.

I calmed myself to say, 'Now, Willie, my heart is at rest.'

'Well, I am glad it is.'

'Did the doctor say you would not get better?'

'Not exactly, — but he looked it.'

After this we thought no more of recovery. We felt it such a comfort to be at liberty to talk together freely of this great event which was at hand, and which concerned us all so deeply.

* Daniel 3:25

He had been left alone with John next day, and took the opportunity of giving him his hens to look after.

John, who had not as yet been told the exact state of things, said, 'Oh, Willie dear, maybe you'll be spared to us yet; and even although your leg has to be taken off, you could be very happy with us. I am so strong, I could wheel you about anywhere; and you and I might have a farm, and I would do all the outside work, and you could do all the head-work.'

His answer was, 'No, John; I'll never be out of this bed again.'

Led Onward

'Oh the grace that hath sought us,
And led us, and brought us,
And shielded us round with its love!'

Family worship was always conducted in the dining-room, with the doors open so that Willie and I might hear and join with the rest of the family. He was all along very sensitive to a heavy tread on the floor, or to any one kneeling carelessly or moving in a chair clumsily; and thus it was impossible for us all to worship together in his room.

On Saturday, sitting beside him as usual, we heard Father pray earnestly that Willie might recover. After the prayer was finished, I sat still in a reverie. He took my hand very gently down from my face, and said, 'Why does Papa keep praying that I may recover? Does he think I will?'

'We will pray on for your recovery so long as you are with us. We would like to get you back, dear boy.'

'Don't you think, Mother, that it must be very teasing to have us all asking that I may get better, when what God is doing is all for our good?'

'Oh, Willie, we are not displeased with our children when they ask in their ignorance for things we must not give them!'

'Still, if they kept on asking, I doubt you would feel a little teased.'

'Willie, would you like to get well again?'

Willie replied slowly, 'I don't know. I can't say. He knows what would be best.'

'But if you got your choice?'

'Oh, you know I can't say, because it might not be the best thing for me. I think I would rather not, now that I have gone so far.'

On Friday his Uncle John came from England to take one night of nursing his old favourite. He was much overcome on finding Willie in the circumstances in which he was, and it was proposed after two hours or so, that his uncle and father should take a walk before dark to Crookston Castle, and get calmed and refreshed for watching beside him during the night. Willie proposed that I should go too, and urged it so much that at last I consented. It was dark before we got home. Willie received us so interestedly, and said to me, 'Mother, I'm so glad you went; you'll not feel it so trying to go the next time. I wanted you to have the first time over. You'll be there often with the children.'

Whilst walking with Uncle John to Crookston, he asked for a photograph of Willie, thus bringing up to our recollection the fact that we had had none taken since he was a little child. He urged us to get one taken at once. Next day a photographer came out. It cost dear Willie much pain to be set up in bed, to have his coat put on and his bed moved a few feet back from the window, so as to let the instrument in next to the light. We were glad to see that he was interested in it himself, and anxious that it should be successful.

In the afternoon, he said to me, 'Mother, can you think of anything else for me to eat than strawberries? I am afraid I am going to tire of them; and then what am I to do, for I know you'll be making me eat something?'

'Well, dear, try and think of something yourself, and I'll get it for you.'

49

'Well the only thing I can think of is a melon, and I think I would like that very much!'

'Oh, well, dear, we must try and get what you can enjoy; but strawberries are better for you than melons. But I daresay a change will do you no harm.'

I was a little concerned as to how a melon was to be brought from the city, three miles off. I left his sister behind, while I went to give baby her bath. When finished, I brought her to Willie, as usual.

When I entered the drawing-room, the first thing my eye fell on was a beautiful melon lying on his pillow! A young man was sitting beside him. Willie laughed when he saw me hardly able to believe my own eyes. I said, 'Willie, dear, I think some One up yonder is thinking about your very smallest want!'

He replied, 'This looks very like it, Mother!'

This young man had worked beside him in his uncle's cotton mill, to which he had gone during the holidays of last summer. After I left the room again, he asked Willie if he would not be sorry to part with the family. Willie said, 'Oh, no; they'll be all cared for, and I'll see them again; but I would have no objection if God would take wee baby with me.'*

 *See page 141

I had been warned that as the disease progressed there would be 'a general disturbance of the nervous system,' 'possibly great irritability,' and a 'strange, peculiar foreboding.' Through all his illness, we never saw a shadow of irritability. The thing which we greatly feared, never came. Perfect peace seemed to keep heart and mind, even when his body was racked with pain. Perhaps the secret of this may have been in something he said to me either on Friday or Saturday. I was fomenting his knee, and whilst doing this, gave him a text which I though would be helpful to him, and spoke a little about it. He seemed to appreciate it, and then said, 'The text, Mother, which has come straight to me — that nobody has given me — is this one, "Call upon Me in the day of trouble; I will deliver thee, and thou shalt glorify Me"' (Psalm 50:15).

In his last letter to his Aunt Catherine in Pennsylvania, he wrote out this text in full to her; and he also wrote it to his Uncle Patrick in California, tying up a little bit of his hair and sending it to each. He did not say anything about himself in these letters. I asked him to tell them about his state of mind, but he said, 'No, Mother; you know I have not been accustomed to do that. I would like you to do it.'

'Well, then, you must tell me what to say.'

'Mother, you know all they would wish to know about this.'

For about a week he had a strange yearning to see these two. We had got word that his aunt was seriously ill; he said one of these days, — 'Oh, I hope the doctors will say to her, 'Go home to Scotland at once! She can't live in this climate!' Then you would just put a bed in that corner there, and nurse us both! Wouldn't that be nice?'

Some one expressed a fear that the next tidings would be that she had died. A look of joy came over his countenance, and looking into my eyes, he said, 'Oh, wouldn't that be nice if she was there when I went?'

I said, 'Ah, Willie, it would be nice for you; but what about her family?'

'Oh, yes; it would be a very sad thing for them. I hope she'll get better for their sakes.'

He spoke of his uncle and aunt being 'so vexed' to get the news about him; they were so far from home. As he spoke of this several times, I said to him once, not to think so sadly of their being away from home; to remember that where they were, was home to them — they had their families and home interests about them, etc.; but when I had finished, he just shook his head sadly, and said, — 'Mother, they are far from their home! Be sure to write them both all about this, and do what you can to keep them from being too much grieved. Write them often, mother!'

On Saturday I was feeling very tired, and he asked me to draw the couch close up beside him and lie down. He took his pillow and put it under my head, kissed me, and then said, 'Now you are to lie there for one hour. I have just been thinking that you said, when you came up from Toward, you felt so worn out with watching and nursing and getting no sleep, that you would just sleep on for a fortnight, to make up! How much sleep have you had? Then you said, after that, you were going for walks with us four. I hope you'll get to keep this last promise, Mother. Do go out on walks with these three (John, Cathie, and Agnes). It will keep them from missing me, and it would be good for you. Mother, I want to ask two things - will you promise not to be vexed?'

'What are they, and then I'll tell you?'

'How much did Regie's funeral cost?' (Regie was his little brother, who had died of scarlet fever in 1874, aged 3 years.)

'Oh, dear, I don't know. What makes you ask that?'

'I just want to know. How many carriages were there?'

'Just grandpapa's, besides the one to carry the little body.'

'Then the other question is, Where will I be buried?'

'Where would you like?'

'Where would you?'

'Beside dear grandpapa and Regie.'

'I think I would like that too; but just promise that I'll lie where all you are to lie. I think Papa doesn't want the Necropolis. I don't like it either; but then it was grandpapa's wish that we should all be in his grave, or he never would have bought so much ground. But I am quite contented to be put anywhere, if only you promise faithfully that I'll not be separated from the rest of our family.'

'I'll promise that, dear. Can you leave it all to us now?'

'Very well.'

'Who should be at my funeral?'

'Whom would you wish?'

'The uncles, aunts, grandmamma, you. Will you be able to go, mother?'

'Yes.'

'Oh, that's nice! I hope you'll keep well, and be able to go with Papa. Then the cousins, and all the children down to James. None younger, Mother, for you could not explain to them.'

After a little he said, 'Mother, I think none of the cousins should be asked; for if one were asked, I would like all to be, and (smiling), if you don't know, I know, that every mourning carriage costs a pound. Now see what a number of carriages would be needed for so many! I think I'll ask grandmamma if she will pay it all! Will you be angry if I do? I would like to do it, and I am sure she would like to do this last thing for me!'

Soon after this, as I sat sewing beside him, after he had looked out of the window for a while, apparently lost in thought, he said, 'The only thing that vexes me about this is, that just when I could have been of some use to Papa and you, I am taken away! You have been paying out, spending money on me till now; and if I had gone to the mill this year, I would have made some money for you, and it would always have been getting more; but here I am, and have never done a thing to help Papa. I am a little sorry about that.'

Something was said about mournings; he said, with a startled look, 'Oh, Mother, I hope you don't mean to say that you have to go into town the first thing after I am away and choose bonnets and dresses, and come home with one of your awful headaches, and then sit down consulting, and sewing and fitting! The very idea is absurd!'

'But, Willie, you would not like it if we did not put on mourning.'

'Why? It will do me no good! Don't think of it!'

'Oh, Willie, it would not be respectful to your memory.'

'Oh, mother! Respectful to my memory! You're vexing me very much thinking of doing such a thing. I wish you would promise me now that you will not. If you want to respect my memory, go out on walks with the others.'

As I still looked doubtful, he seemed a little vexed, and said, 'You might put a band on the boys' arms, and the girls' too. Papa will have a band on his hat, and you are always in black. Do not do more. You have had more than enough of work lately. I want you to get rest when I leave you.'

Shortly afterwards, he said, 'Mother, what is that in here?' He tapped his chest. 'Put down your ear and listen.' I heard a strange sound in his chest, and as he looked for an answer, I said, 'Well, dear, it's just another messenger from the King of kings, to say that you are wanted very soon up yonder.'

He gave a little nod, and said, 'I thought so.'

His Uncle James came on Sabbath and watched with him through the night. When his father came down in the early morning to relieve him, Uncle James told Willie playfully that this was quite upsetting their plans, that they had not counted upon his leaving them in this way, and said some other things pleasing to him to hear.

His father was standing at the window, looking out on the lovely prospect, and made the remark, 'We are not to forget that He who made this world so beautiful, is the One who is preparing for us the home beyond.'

Willie said heartily, 'Yes, Papa; and that will be a good deal better than being made a partner in the mill!'

In the evening his father was sitting alone with him, when he suddenly asked the rather startling question, 'Papa, where are you going to bury me?'

'I'll bury you in my heart, my boy!'

He smiled and said, 'Oh, I know that; but you cannot bury this old leg of mine there, and what are you going to do with it?'

'He shall change the body of our humiliation, that it may be fashioned like unto the body of His glory.'

'Oh, I know that, too; but He is not going to do that all at once. Tell me, where are you going to put it till then?'

'Where would you like?'

'Oh, I don't know. Sometimes I think at the end of that long row of Riddells in the quiet churchyard in Eskdalemuir. But of course, that's impossible; we could not all be there, and I want us all to be together.'

'Say where you would like, and then we'll carry out your wish if it is possible.'

'Oh, no; don't ask me! What if I say the top of Buacholain! That hill behind Toward. Oh, how delightful the thought of being laid to rest in Cathcart Cemetery, too, though. I don't mind. Mother has promised we'll be all together. It would be nice to be beside dear wee Regie and grandpapa, if we were all gathered there.'

A few days before the end, when his Uncle Joseph was leaving, he said, — 'Mother, have you settled about the grave yet?'

'No.'

'Well, you haven't much time now. You should speak to Uncle Joseph just now.'

I said, 'Willie, I know that you will be quite pleased with whatever Papa and I do with that dear, precious body that has been such a care and such a pleasure to us.'

'Oh, yes!' he said, with a pleasant smile, and never again referred to the subject again.

Thoughts in View of Home

'Dark streams are still dividing
Between my Lord and me;
Time's midnight hills are hiding
The land I fain would see.

'But oh, the wondrous morrow!
Life without pain or loss, —
The saints without their sorrow,
And Christ without the Cross!'

On Sabbath evening his father read to him the end of the second part of Bunyan's *Pilgrim's Progress*. When he came to read about the post bringing the message to Mr. Honest to be ready to present himself before the Lord at His Father's house against this day seven nights, Willie interrupted, 'Papa, I think I have got that message. Do you think I'll be here longer than that?'

'Well, my boy, I do not think you will.'

'Oh, I am very glad! I would not like if it were to be long. You might take an opportunity soon to read that to grandmamma and John. Will you, Papa?'

His Uncle Joseph sat with him the first part of the night, and when I came to him in the morning, he said, in answer to my inquiries, —

'Oh, yes; I got such a sweet sleep! I never saw anything like it! I was so afraid, after you went upstairs to bed, that I should not get to sleep again, and I felt so tired! I could get no rest, and I thought I could not live if I did not get a little ease and sleep. So dear Uncle Joseph knelt beside me and said that text – you know it, Mother, — 'If two of you shall agree,' and prayed that I might get a little sleep, and in less than five minutes I was asleep!'

His uncle, when leaving on Monday morning, asked John to accompany him to the mill. Willie watched them going down the hill, and as 'going with Uncle Joseph' was one of the bright bits of life to him, I felt sorry that he should have observed them, and was thinking how I could best call his eyes and his thoughts away from it, when he surprised me by turning to me and saying, 'Mother, John had better take my good hat to wear now. He likes it, and it fits him; and then he can keep his good one for church. I'll not need it again and it's a pity to have it upstairs useless.

'Mother, you must remember my new shoes have only been on once, the day I came up from Toward. They won't do for John; I wonder if they would fit Willie Ross. The first time he comes out, you might let him try them!'

He said these two things evidently without a thought of regret.

His father was going into town, and asked me to see what Willie would like him to bring for him.

'I don't know, Mother.'

'Oh, say something, Willie.'

'I can't, Mother; I don't know anything to say!'

'Dear me, Willie, is there nothing you want? Papa would like to bring something; say anything.'

He laughed, and said, 'I really don't know anything to say.'

'Well, Willie, you must be a very well off boy!'

'Indeed, I am! The only thing I want is you, and when I haven't you, Papa; and when I haven't Papa, you!'

His pet hens were passing his window in a little group. He made some remarks about how nice they looked. I said, 'Ah, Willie, I'll often see them passing when my boy is away, and I'll feel sorrowful and heavy-hearted.'

'Oh, I hope not, Mother! Try to enjoy what I enjoyed and had so much pleasure in; and let dear John have pleasure in them. I have given them to him. You know, I'll have far better!'

We were both admiring the exceeding beauty of the view from his bed. I said, 'I am afraid, that after you're away, I'll feel the loveliness all around quite oppressive. I doubt I'll not like to live here.'

He seemed surprised, and said, 'Oh, Mother! What a thing to say! You could not vex me more than by allowing my going away to lessen your pleasure and enjoyments. I would like you to be as happy as I have been here.'

'And have you been happy here, dear?'

'Oh, very; I could scarcely have been more so! I would like all of you to be the same, although I am away!'

His leg required a fomentation with hot olive oil and a preparation of laudanum every hour; when the pain was very great, we did it a little oftener. We sang occasionally, repeated passages of Scripture to him, and talked with him 'of Jesus and His love,' and so helped these hours of suffering to pass as profitably and as pleasantly as we could. His grateful spirit in the midst of so much suffering was very touching. Sometimes it was impossible for us to keep back the burning tears when attending to the leg; and he was always so ready with a kiss and a kindly pat, and a word of comfort, such as, 'Oh, it's not so bad,' or 'Oh, mother, it might be a great deal worse.' Once, when I was a little overcome at the thought of his leaving us so soon, he said quite brightly, 'Mother, didn't you think that John and I might go to New Zealand? Well, I am not going so far – and I'll be quite safe.'

He was wearying a little for John to come back from the mill, and this led him on to speak with great surprise and gratification of what his uncles had planned for him. He had not expected it. From that, he went on to speak anxiously about John, and ended by saying, 'Oh, I wish Uncle Joseph would just take John instead of me. He's so nice! I know uncle would like him far better than me, if he only knew him.'

'Is he so nice?' I said, laughing.

'Oh, he's awful nice; you can't help liking John!'

Our next-door neighbour had said she would like to see him. Willie was eager to say good-bye to her, 'She is soon away to Iona for a month and she has been so kind and thoughtful, making so many nice things for me. I'll not be here when she comes back.'

When John returned, he sat beside him and kept him interested in all he had seen at the mill, and told him what his Uncle Joseph had done. Seeing Willie suffering very great pain, he said, sympathetically, 'Dear Willie, is your leg very sore?'

He answered, 'Oh, John, it's been an awful leg! Oh, it has been an awful leg! I cannot tell you what a leg it has been!'

'What is the pain like, dear?'

'Well, you know these sheets of lead the plumbers work with? Can you imagine what it would be to have yards and yards of that rolled tight round your leg? Then, besides that, it has a queer sort of pain which is indescribable!!'

He gave his keys to John. His bunch of keys had always been a great matter to him, and it was touching to see how easily, although  interestedly, he now gave them up. He explained what each key opened (I was sitting by, sewing), and as John never spoke in answer, he gave a quick look up in his face, and when he saw the sorrowful, broken—hearted expression on his brother's face, he threw his arm round his neck, kissed him very heartily, saying, 'Poor John, don't look that way. You know I'll have far better.'

His leg was now growing at the rate of an inch or an inch and a half in girth, above the knee, every day. It got a little discoloured latterly. All that we gave to nourish our darling boy seemed just to nourish this dreadful growth instead, and when John offered him some food, in my absence, he said, 'Oh, John, you don't know how hard it is for me to keep taking these things, that I hate at any rate, when I know it only keeps me a little longer away from Jesus; but then God teaches Mother and Father to keep feeding me till He sends for me; and of course I must obey Father and Mother, and take what they give me.'

I said, 'Willie, what a bundle of your stockings there is lying for me to mend! I'll be sitting alone darning them when you are away, and I'll be thinking how I used to scold you for being at your gymnastics in your stocking soles, you made such big holes; and then I'll be so vexed, and you won't be here to comfort me.'

He said nothing for a little, and then, 'Mother, I think you should get a seamstress to do them all. I know you will vex yourself over them, and I don't want you to be vexed thinking of me. I'll be so much happier and better every way, at the very time you are sitting mourning over me, than I would be if I were here. Try, Mother, to realize that, and it will stop your crying.'

About a quarter of an hour after, he said, 'Mother, I think the best way about the stockings will be to give them all away, and then they'll be out of your sight. They don't fit John, and it will be a long time before James can use them, and there are none of them very new; so just do that, will you, Mother?'

Then Willie added with a thoughtful tone, 'Mother, do you think we will be allowed to see our friends on earth, when we are in heaven?'

'Well, dear, what do you think yourself?'

'I do not know. I don't think it — I don't think I would like it!'

'Well, I don't think so either; but that's only an opinion. This I know, that till we meet again, Jesus will never be out of your sight, and we can never be out of His sight; and that is a very sure link between us. Certainly, if you see us, you'll like it.'

'I wonder if we will be sent to earth to do anything. I mean, I wonder if I may be allowed to come and be with you at times.'

'I wonder that too, dear; but that's really of no importance to us at all. You will certainly be satisfied with all the arrangements of that bright home; you can ask no more.'

He could never fall asleep now unless the one in charge held his hand. When I was writing a note, he said, 'Are you nearly finished? I feel a little sleepy.'

'Well, dear, just sleep,' I said, to see what he would say. He smiled, and said, 'I could never go to sleep if you sat there.'

'Why?'

'Oh, I can give you no reason for it. I only know I couldn't. You must at least come and give me the start, and if I fall asleep, just leave me; but please, mother, be in your place again when I awake. I get a little startled when you are not, and it makes the pain of my leg almost more than I can bear.'

'Oh, Willie, I wish I had got that leg instead of you.'

He said so earnestly, 'Well, mother, that is one thing I do not wish. Oh, how thankful I am that it is not you that has got this leg! What would we all have done?'

I said something about feeling too weary, and having a wish that I might get away with him. He looked anxiously in my face and said, 'Oh no, dear mother! You must not speak that way, nor allow yourself to think that way. It would be an awful thing for you to be taken away just now. I know you are very weary, but God will strengthen you, and cheer you too, after I am away. I hope I'll not see you for thirty years yet.'

He was stroking my cheeks kindly, as he said this seemingly unkind thing. I said, 'Oh, Willie, thirty years is a long time.'

'Well, maybe if your work is done in twenty years, you'll get away; but I hope you'll be left to see every one of us in the right way. You know I'll be there, and Regie; and I do hope we'll all be there together, and not one lost. You must lead them all to Jesus before you come. Remember you have eleven, a whole eleven, Mother, to train for Jesus, and care for their bodies as well.'

When settling the room for the night, he said, 'Mother, if I am to get a nurse for the nights, do you think Papa would be agreeable to let me have your photograph that is in the dining-room hung up there?' Willie pointed to where a photograph of Holman Hunt's 'Light of the World' was hung on the wall. 'I think when I would waken with a start from my short sleeps, and see your face at once, I would not feel so much that I was handed over to a stranger.'

I felt troubled at his saying this, and reminded him that the picture represented how much Jesus could do for him.

'Yes, I know that; but I am like you in that – I don't like pictures of Christ.'

'But,' I said, 'the story told in the picture is a very touching one.'

'Yes,' he replied slowly, 'but He does not need to stand at my heart door! But if Papa would not like it, never mind. I just was thinking I had got so accustomed to look up and see your face or dear father's, that if I saw a stranger's there, I might not be able to go over to sleep again.'

Five minutes was about the duration of his sleeps, and then a twinge of pain in his leg startled him again out of his sleep.

'If you settle to get a nurse, Mother, you or Papa might go to an institution where there are a great number, and make them all pass before you. Get the wee-est, thinnest, and lightest in the place; notice if they walk lightly, or if they use their heels chiefly. You know, a nurse would not be so careful to remember as you all are, and I would not like to tell her.'

On Tuesday morning, about 4 a.m., I came down to relieve my husband, bringing Willie's usual cup of tea. The venetian blinds were all down, but outside it was so bright that one felt as if in a shaded room in a palace of gold.

After handing him his cup, I said, 'Willie, dear, I think I'll draw up this blind and let in a little of the brightness of this bonny world you are going from so soon!'

We were very careful never to make the slightest noise suddenly, or touch him or his bed unexpectedly, or change the light without warning, as these added greatly to his pain.

He replied, 'No, I can't see out now. Oh, well, I daresay you may; it can come in. I thought I was away last night to see the brightness, mother, the brightness of the Father's face!'

'You have but a few more steps now till you see the King in His beauty, my dear boy.'

'Oh, I am very glad: the sooner the better!'

At breakfast time, a basket of newly—gathered strawberries was handed in, sent by kind and attentive friends in the neighbourhood. I had noticed with a sorrowful heart that he was gradually leaving off everything. Strawberries had been for a length of time almost the only thing he cared for. I persuaded him to take one, and when offering him a second, he closed his eyes, and said solemnly, 'No, dear mother, don't ask me. I am going to eat of the fruit of the Tree of Life, whose leaves are for the healing of the nations. I want no more.'

In the forenoon, when suffering intense pain in his leg, I tried various things in the hope that he might be relieved; but this time failing utterly, I stood up at last and just looked at him, and said, 'And is this really Willie Riddell?' His answer was a striking one.

'No, it's not Willie Riddell; at least, it's not to be Willie Riddell any more. It's to be a new name now, written on a white stone, which no man knoweth save he that receiveth it.'

A solemn calm seemed to steal over him as he said these words, and – to my inexpressible relief – he fell asleep. Further on in the day he pointed to a photograph of his mother, taken with hands folded on an open Bible and looking downward on it, and said, 'Mother what book is it you are reading in that photograph?'

'A Bible.'

'Then you are reading with folded hands, "Father, I will that those whom Thou hast given Me be with Me where I am, that they may behold My glory." Will you remember that after, mother dear?'

He never mentioned the word death, but always spoke of the time which was now drawing so near, as 'after.'

Consideration for Others

'A thoughtful love,
Through constant watching wise,
And a heart at leisure from itself,
To soothe and sympathise.'

Something was said about Toward. I said sadly,
'Oh, that Toward! How can I go back there
again, and no Willie!'

'Why, Mother?'

'Because you were so fond of it, and had so
much pleasure in going there.'

'I think that is a very good reason for your
going. You should go happily when you think
how very happy I always was there.'

'I suppose you were very happy there.'

'Oh, very! I have been happy in all my homes;
but I think I may say I have been happiest in
the Toward home. I hope you will not think
of giving it up! Papa, I wish you would make

75

Mother not think and feel this way! Mother,' he said earnestly, 'although you feel it a little trying for a time or two, you must go for the sake of the children. You've no idea what happiness it is to them; and for the sake of their health, I hope you'll not give up Toward, although I am not there.'

After prayer with him on another occasion, he said, 'I think we do not ask enough that God may be glorified. We are always asking things for ourselves; but man's chief end is to glorify God.'

His father proposed to write and give up an engagement to assist at the communion at Colintraive, Kyles of Bute, a week after the following Sabbath. Willie said, 'No, Papa dear, don't do that; I'll be away, I am quite sure, before that. I want you to go and take dear mother with you; she is so fond of the Kyles, and you'll both need a rest after this.'

He spoke many times about my being kept so much away from the children, he thought it must be so dull for them. I remember his saying, 'But it can only be for a little while now, and then you will get attending to them rightly. I hope God will strengthen you and dear Papa for the work you have to do, after this time of trouble is over. I hope neither of you will be ill after this. You must try and get a day or two of rest somewhere after I am away. I think Helensburgh is the best place for you to get rest in, Mother. There are no children, and everything is so quiet and orderly and comfortable. Then there's the phaeton, and you like a pony phaeton so much.'

Sometimes he would hear baby cry. 'Oh, that poor wee baby! I am very vexed about keeping you so much from her; but I need you so much.'

On Tuesday, late in the evening, his cousin Edwin and I were standing talking together in the window beside Willie. Suddenly I remembered that some one had said James could not be found for dinner or for tea. I asked Edwin if James had turned up.

'No, he has been away all day; nobody knows anything about him. Does he do this often?'

'No,' I said; 'he never goes away alone. Willie, do you know of his ever having gone off in this way?'

'No; I never knew of his going away to any place without John or me.'

'Oh,' I said, 'I wish he were home; it's getting dark!'

Edwin said, 'Never mind, aunt; I'll go and look for him.'

Willie said quietly, 'Mother, this is your day of trouble; aren't you troubled?'

'Yes, indeed I am.'

'Come and pray then. He wants you to do that always when you are in trouble. Pray that James may be brought home.'

He smiled expressively when he heard James's voice soon afterwards in the lobby.

It had been arranged that I should sit up the first part of Tuesday night with him, but the sight of his constant suffering (he could not keep his head down on his pillow beyond a few minutes at a time, and the relief he got by rising on his elbow was but for a moment), and my inability to help except by a verse of Scripture, became to me so intolerable, that I had to go up and awake dear Papa, and ask him to come and sit beside me.

As I passed the open doors of so many sleepers, even though I knew it was with many of them a 'sleeping for sorrow,' I felt keenly what a lonely thing suffering is; and the words came to me, 'Couldst thou not watch with Me one hour?'

About an hour after, his father made me go up to bed, and I too slept for some hours very soundly.

On Wednesday, he said to me rather unexpectedly, 'Mother, do you think it will be very sore just at the end?'

'We cannot say anything about that, dear. No one has ever come back to tell us; but you don't need to think about that. The same One who has led you so wonderfully through this terrible illness, will be with you then. I can say that much; so there's no need to fear. Besides, many seem just to have fallen asleep as usual, and never wakened here again. Perhaps at the very end there may not be so much pain as you have had these days.'

'Oh, Mother, how I should like to fall asleep, and wake up in His arms! I am a little afraid of the very end; if it's sorer than this, I don't know how I'll be able to bear it!'

His father then said: 'Willie, we'll leave it all to Jesus. He has cared for us very tenderly up till now, and He'll care for you at the very end.' This seemed to set his mind completely at rest, and this shadow fled away.

Baby cried; Willie looked vexed, and said, 'Oh, that sweet wee pet, I am so vexed keeping its mother from it! I am very sorry I cannot have her in this room now!'

'Oh, baby is well off, Willie; all babies cry now and again.'

He shook his head.

'A baby can't be 'well off' without its mother.'

'She has a nurse.'

'A nurse is not a mother! But this can't last long; I'll soon be away, and then you'll just make up for this. Poor wee pet! She must wonder why you are not keeping her as you used to do.'

He expressed a wish that he might get away soon, and asked me to feel if his feet were not beginning to get cold. I said 'Oh, Willie, you forget how we shall miss you when you go. I feel vexed when you speak as if you did not think of that at all.'

'Mother, it will be well every way when the end comes; not for me alone I mean, but for you, and for baby, and for the whole house. You should be at the dinner table just now: it's your right place.'

'This is my right place just now, Willie.'

'Oh, well, I daresay it is. But this would not do to continue; the others need you, the servants need you, and dear baby is not getting the care we all got at her age.'

'Well, Willie, it will be a great sorrow to me when you leave me!'

'I know that, mother dear; but you'll be comforted by thinking I'm all well now, and

wee baby will fill your hands
and be a great pleasure to
you. You'll have to take her
out on your walks, and you'll
soon get over this time of
sorrow.'

'Papa, you and
Mother must just
keep telling the
children about
Jesus. They forget
so easily; and oh, I hope none of us will be
lost! It would be so nice if we were all there, in
heaven every one — that would be thirteen!'

'Quite a little congregation,' his father said.

'Yes; it would be very nice; and you and
Mother — that would be fifteen!'

'Willie,' I said, 'if I had known you were going
to leave me so soon, I would not have drilled
you as I did. When I look back and think of all
the scoldings and punishings and faultfindings,
I wish I had not trained you so much, and just
left you alone.'

'Ah! but that would have been very wrong,
mother. It was all needed.'

'Well, if it was all needed, the spirit in which
I often found fault with you was not needed, and
was far from being what it should have been.'

81

'Oh, mother dear, I wonder you were so patient, for I have been a most aggravating boy.'

John had been spending some hours sorrowfully in Willie's room, arranging his things. He brought me a paper and asked me to look at it. I found it was my rules and arrangements for him, written out, and at the end this prayer: 'O Jesus, enable me to keep these rules, if Thou dost approve of them, and do Thou keep me in remembrance of them. Make me walk in Thy light. Amen.'

The rules of which he speaks were rendered necessary owing to the state of his health. The eagerness of his disposition made him liable to forget them, and I had said that I would not reckon it obedience if I required to be continually reminding him of them.

'Willie, dear, do you know that John and James have taken possession of your room? They have moved their things into it, and sleep there now.'

'Oh, yes, I know; they spoke to me about it before they did it. Don't you think it a very good idea — for afterwards, I mean? They would not like to move into it again, and they would not like my room standing empty!'

Cousin Jeanie offered to take three of the children to Helensburgh. James was specially invited. In his hearing, Willie said earnestly, 'No, not James; he is too good a boy to be sent away! Send Sophie please mother and perhaps Janie and Etie. I can't bear to hear Sophie crying when she is put out of my room, and I am getting too weak now to have her beside me. The other two wonder I don't speak more to them; so these three are better away now. James is no trouble in the house. Do you hear that, Jim ?'

83

When they were ready to go, I brought Sophie in my arms to say 'Goodbye' to him. He made fun with her about her gloves and boots. She never had had on boots before. He turned up her little feet, pretended to look surprised, and said, 'Oh, what a lady! Boots and gloves!' She said, 'Not touch my wee boots. Naughty boy for touching my good boots!'

Willie said, 'Don't say that little sis! Give me a kiss, and say I'm a good boy; I'll be away when you come back!'

Ettie came very gently to his side next to say 'Goodbye.' My attention was called off for a moment, and when I looked again, Ettie (six years of age) had her arms clasped tightly round his neck, giving him a hearty hug! It was with great difficulty I got the little impetuous being disengaged, and he lay back on his pillow half-laughing, half-crying. I was greatly alarmed, and after seeing him right, I made as if to go after Ettie to give her a rebuke; he put out his hand to stop me: 'Don't, mother; it's just the love of her heart; and it was my fault — I put out my arms for her. Besides, it can't happen again — she'll not be back!'

Cousin Jeanie, after saying goodbye, said through her tears, 'Willie, I want to come back.'

'When?'

'Friday, if your father will allow me, or Saturday.'

'Not later, Jeanie.'

Someone remarked that it was kind and thoughtful of the boys in the neighbourhood that they did not play football now in the evenings. I said, 'Willie, what shall I think of football now?'

He smiled and said, 'Now, Mother, I was quite sure you would be thinking that way! You must not. Let the boys enjoy it. I like it still! It's not really so rough as it looks. Now, mother, you know that there's no such thing as an accident; this leg might have come hundreds of other ways. It has just been the messenger to me.'

Edwin, his cousin, sat with him part of the night. Willie spoke of his kindness and attention, and said, 'and he prayed so nicely for you and Papa.'

His pulse all this week kept about one hundred and thirty.

He consulted with his father about laying out the pound he had got from his grandmamma at the beginning of his illness, in buying little books to give to those who had shown him so much love and care.

Up till that day I had always brought baby in, night and morning, after bathing her, and before she was quite dressed, and laid her in Willie's arms. This was a pleasure to him (and to her!) which seemed to lift him quite above his pain for a few minutes. When he would hear by her happy little crow that she was coming, it was touching to see how the fading face lighted up, and the arms were formed into a cradle for her in a moment.

His Uncle Joseph had hung a text-card at the head of his bed. Walter (eighteen months) had made sundry efforts to get hold of it; so Willie said, 'Mother, will you give this card to dear wee Walter when I am done with it, and tell him some day how he struggled to get it into his wee fists over Willie's head. Put it aside for him.'

I handed it to him, saying, 'Will you write on it?' He held the pen a minute, and then said, 'What shall I write?'

'Write his name, and tell him to be sure to meet you in heaven.'

'No, Mother; I can't do that. I have never liked that, as if I were the chief person there.

'Well, then, dear, just write a text or anything you please.'

I was playing with Walter on my knee. He wrote, and then handed it to me to put away. I was pleased and touched to find the following written on it: *'Dear Walter, read this card with care, and pray that God will show you the way to Himself, through Jesus, who died that you might be saved.* "Oh taste and see that God is good." I have found Him good.'

He wrote on a pretty little copy of the New Testament, 'To my sweet little Edith May,' handed it to me, and said, 'Put it away, Mother, till she is old enough to know about this.'

One day, speaking of a young friend, about whose spiritual welfare he felt deeply concerned, and whom he wished his father to deal with, he said to me, 'There is one thing I forgot. I wanted you to tell Papa to take Robbie on his knee. That is the way his own papa does. And then, you see, he would not feel so much to speak to Papa, his face would be kind of turned away!'

I wanted him to take a little bit of peach. He said, 'No; but I should like a little bit of black sugar again just the size of a pin-head, Mother.' I expressed surprise at this, and he said, 'Oh, you can't tell what a good thing it is for the mouth, when it is so bad as mine is now.'

'Is your mouth sore, dear?'

He seemed to remember then that he had never spoken of it, and for answer he lifted my finger and put it into his mouth, and looked to see the effect on my face. It was as if I had put it into hot sand. I could not speak, and he said quite interestedly, 'Mother, it's well for you to know this – it might be useful for some other person, especially if they were poor; for you see I have everything, and I find there is nothing helps the dryness of my mouth like a very small bit of black sugar laid on my tongue. I don't think I would speak if it weren't for that. Everything else seems just to dry up as it enters my mouth.'

Perfect Peace

'Peace, perfect peace, with sorrows surging round?
On Jesus' bosom nought but calm is found.

'Peace, perfect peace, death shadowing us and ours?
Jesus has vanquished death and all its powers.'

In the afternoon he lay looking out towards the city with such a calm, pleasant countenance, that I felt very much impressed with the deep perfect peace he was enjoying. At length I said, 'Willie, you seem always to be very much at rest in your mind and heart. Have you never any doubts or fears?'

'No, I can't say I have; I feel quite at rest.'

About half an hour later, he turned anxiously to me, saying, 'Mother, can there by any mistake?' I hesitated, and he added, 'I mean in thinking I am His?'

We went over together the grounds of his trust and confidence, and he and I were alike satisfied; but his father coming in just as we had finished, I told him what we were speaking about. I felt greatly relieved by his coming in at that moment. I felt so afraid that I might have said anything to mislead. His father quickly took in the state of things, and spoke pretty nearly as follows: 'Well, Willie, is there any mistake about this, that in yourself you are a lost and helpless sinner?'

'No; there can be no mistake about that.'

'Then can there be any mistake about this, that Jesus "came to seek and to save the lost," and that "this Man receiveth sinners"?'

'No, Papa; there can be no mistake about that.'

'Then can there be any mistake about this, that you are giving yourself now to Him as a lost and helpless sinner, and leaving yourself to Him to save you?'

'No, Papa; I know I am doing that.'

'Then is there any mistake about this, that He has said, that those who do that "shall never perish, neither shall any pluck them out of His hand"?'

'I see; it's just trusting it all to Jesus.'

'Then it just comes to this, that if Jesus shall keep His word, we are perfectly safe; and that there can be no mistake, unless He break it.'

Someone asked to be remembered in his prayers. He assented in a sort of anxious way, and added, 'I am such a young, inexperienced Christian myself.'

I asked once more if I could not attend to his leg. He smiled, and said, 'No; it's not very sore today.' Pointing to his chest he said, 'I have more pain here, today than I have in my leg.'

He was much pleased with his father's purchase of books, and especially with some textbooks.

'Papa, I am afraid you did not buy all these with my money?'

'Oh, yes, dear; it was very little more than the pound.'

'Ah, but I did not want you to give a penny more than what I had to give.'

'Ah, but, Willie,' I said, 'you're forgetting that Papa has seven or eight shillings of your own, keeping for you.'

'Oh, so you have, Papa; that's nice!'

He had much pleasure in writing some names immediately; and he had to take farewell of several aunts and cousins. He had wearied much for his Cousin Warren, born the same day as him. Several times he expressed anxiety about him, and a great desire that he might be saved. As he was long of coming, he said he feared he would be too weak to speak to him soon, but he would like very much to see him once more.

On Thursday evening I said, 'Well, I see Warren coming up the hill; are you glad?'

'Oh, I wish he had come sooner. I feel so tired! I don't think I'll be able to speak to him now. I want to see him alone, mother.' We arranged that Warren should take my place by his bedside while we were at worship.

When Warren came down, I went up expecting to find our dear boy very much exhausted; but he was looking eagerly for me (the tiredness all forgotten!), asked me to shut the door, then said, 'I wish you or Papa would speak to Warren tonight. I think he wants to be Christ's, but does not know how.'

'Well, dear, Papa has most skill in directing seeking ones, so I'll ask him to do it.'

'Very well, and come you back and pray with me, while Papa is speaking to him. Pray that God may give Papa the right thing to say, and that Warren may understand and take Christ as his Saviour.'

As I rose from my knees, he kissed me and thanked me warmly. He then went on to speak most earnestly about his cousin, beseeching me to care for him. 'Try and think of him just as you have thought of your own Willie. Bring him about the house as much as ever you can; will you, mother? I wonder if you could take both Edward and Warren always from Saturday till Monday? Would it be too much for you? I know they would make as little work as ever they could. I know you have enough to care for; but they have no Mother to care for them. Aunt Emily will be so thankful and pleased if she knows you are caring for her boys and helping them to come to where she is.'

Dear Aunt Emily had been called away from her home and her family, very unexpectedly, six years before, leaving five boys.

Willie continued, 'You know Warren has nothing but lodgings and the office, and you know how I would hate that. I think he would listen to you about other things, when he sees you so kind. Oh, I wouldn't like Warren to be lost; we've been such friends, and he has always been so very kind to me.'

'Willie, dear, you'll not bind me down to do anything after you are away? I might not see my way to do what you have asked me.'

'Oh, no, Mother! I wasn't meaning to bind you by any promise, but just do what you can for him.'

On Friday morning he wearied till the household got astir. He expressed anxiety lest Warren should miss the train, and wanted us to have worship before he needed to leave. He asked for a book that he might choose a Psalm. I gave him his father's book, and asked him to mark it. He chose the 103rd, and wrote the tune he wanted sung to it alongside the verses, 'Such pity as a father hath.' His father had told him on Thursday evening, when I was absent, that it was cancer. He was not in any way moved by it. He now asked me to take off the last wrapping. When doing this, the tears blinded my eyes so that I could not see to undo the fastenings. He smiled at me and said, 'I'm sure you needn't be vexed to get done with that troublesome leg, dear mother!'

I asked him why he had never asked for Professor Macleod's opinion.

He said, as if thinking, 'Did I not? I never noticed that I had not asked you.'

'Are you glad we did not tell you it was cancer till now?'

'Oh, yes, it was as well. It was very kind of you.'

'Did you ever think it might be cancer?'

'Never.'

I was sitting beside him in the forenoon, when he startled me by saying, 'Mother, if the doctors want to examine my leg 'after,' would you let them?'

'Why?'

'Because they have not known very well about it, I think; and it might be of use to some other poor fellow. They might learn how it first began, and how it went on, and what they could have done to ease the pain; but would you let them?'

'Should I ?'

'Oh, yes, I think you should. Just see that it is sent back in time; you understand me, mother!'

'I am afraid I would not like it.'

'Oh, you needn't mind, Mother. You know our bodies — my body — will crumble to dust; but God is going to restore it again, and make it a glorious body like unto His, and you'll never see a mark!'

His chest gradually became very painful, and it was touching to hear him say, 'Oh, how good it is of God to have taken away the pain of my leg when my chest is so bad, and my cough so distressing!'

He wrote a number of inscriptions on the little books, and asked me not to have them lying about, as some could not be given until after. He seemed to feel it a sacred thing. I handed him his father's Bible, saying, 'Write something nice there for dear Papa.'

'Oh, I am afraid I'll spoil it, my hand is so weak.'

'No fear of that; your papa will often have to bury his sorrow in his heart, and go forth to comfort others, and many times it will be trying enough to do this.'

'Well, if you think it will be a help to him, I'll do it. Dear father! it will need to be all comforting texts for him. I know he'll miss me.'

He wrote: '*Dear father, God has said: "I am He that comforteth you." "As one whom his mother comforteth, so I will comfort thee." "Blessed be God! who comforteth us..." (2 Corinthians 1: 3—5).*

'*He is a dear, kind Lord. - W.E.R., Aug. 2nd 1883.*'

He asked me to turn up the last of these texts, and give him the exact words; but he was too weak to write more. When I handed him my church hymn-book, he said, 'What shall I write?'

'Oh, a nice text.'

He gave a smile, and looking roguishly at me, said, 'I think it will have to be, "Little mother, keep yourself from idols!" What he did write on my hymn-book I found to be, 'To my darling mother: a memento of happy days, both past and yet to come.'

'Oh, I am so thankful we have not needed to get a nurse. You see, mother, you have been made able for it; and you'll try and get a rest somewhere at once, and you'll be all right again. I began by being your baby, and I am just ending your baby.'

I said, 'I am afraid it is a little selfish of us asking you to write these things, when it hurts you so much; and the getting of your photograph taken, too. I am afraid I'll blame myself after you are away.'

'Oh, no, mother. If it's a pleasure to them all, I am glad to do it. It's but a little thing, but it's all I can do for Jesus now.'

He suffered great pain in his chest all Friday night. When sitting sympathising with him, he asked, 'Mother, who were with Jesus at the cross? I mean of His disciples and friends? Was there none of the disciples but John?'

'Well, really, dear, I can't remember at this moment; but whenever this bad turn is over a little, I'll read to you Farrar's account of it.'

'Oh, thank you! That'll be nice.'

The attack only passed off as he fell asleep from exhaustion. He must have learned all about that in his Redeemer's immediate presence, for we never spoke of it again. He seemed to be asleep, but was still in sore distress. To assist his poor wasted lungs a little, I slipped my hand under his pillow and raised it very gently. I heard him say, as if dreaming, 'I'll soon be up now, but I'm very tired; but I'm nearly in now... to the city-set-on-a-hill ... which hath ... foundations ... and there'll be... no... mistake.'

His Uncle Joseph relieved me after getting two hours' sleep. When sitting quietly beside him, he heard him say, 'No, thank you.'

Joseph said, 'Do you wish anything, Willie?'

'No; I thought you were offering me something. I'll soon have all I require.'

He was sympathising with him in one of his breathless turns. His reply was, 'He knows how much I can bear, and will not send more.' He had a very bad turn about 3 a.m. His father and I were brought back to be beside him along with Joseph. At four we thought it must be the end approaching. He asked me to sing, as we were supporting him in bed, his verse, which he had 'got' in his illness in 1875.

> *'Into Thine hands I do commit*
> *My spirit, for Thou art He,*
> *O Thou Jehovah, God of truth,*
> *Thou hast redeemed me.'* – Psalm 31:5.

Infact sometime before this his father had asked him, 'Willie, when did you begin first to trust in the Lord Jesus?'

'Oh,' he said, 'it is a good while ago. You remember the verse you gave me when we were all ill with fever, "Into Thine hands,"? I gave myself to Jesus then, and many times since, but I was often led away again. But for some time past, He has been keeping me from being led away ... I cannot help trusting him.'

After the reading of this verse of Scripture Willie closed his eyes reverently, as if singing along with us and giving himself up to God, although not audibly. When we finished, he signed to us to sing it again. None of us could command ourselves sufficiently, but my dear husband managed to say it over, and we noticed that Willie's lips moved again, as if repeating it with his father. Joseph said, 'When thou passest through the waters, I will be with thee.' These are the waters you are passing through now, Willie.

'Are they? They're not so bad, not nearly so bad, as they might have been. He is soon coming now. They shall not overflow me.'

His father added, '"When thou walkest through the fire, thou shalt not be burnt."'

'Well, if this is the fire, He must be keeping it back from hurting me.'

It was a strangely solemn and blessed time to us three watchers. Joseph wrote of it 'as one of the hours of heaven upon earth; the light of eternal day seemed to be dawning, and the veil drawn aside a little, to give us a glimpse of the land (to us) afar off.'

After a time of sore distress, in which it was evident he was being upheld by the mighty God of Jacob, he recovered a little, and became able to lie down again on his pillow, and speak sweetly and soothingly to us.

About 5 a.m. Willie asked that he and Uncle Joseph might have a last cup of tea together. When I brought his little tray to his side, I handed him his cup and prepared to assist him a little. He looked into my eyes surprisedly, that I should not have helped his uncle first. He waited, and then I understood, and said, 'Oh, I see; you want Uncle Joseph to take it with you!'

'Of course; that's the pleasure of it.'

I set a chair close to his side, and put a cup into Uncle Joseph's hand, and Willie looked so sweetly and reverently to him to ask a blessing.

Father did so, and when they had sipped their tea, talking together meanwhile, he put down his cup, saying pleasantly, 'Now that's my last cup of tea with you, Uncle Joseph.' He used to enjoy having 'a cup of tea with Uncle Joseph,' at the mill and elsewhere occasionally. We then sang the hymn —

A mind at perfect peace with God -
Oh, what a word is this!
A sinner reconciled through blood -
This, this indeed is peace!

By nature and by practice, far -
How very far ! - from God;
Yet now by grace brought nigh to Him
Through faith in Jesus blood.

So nigh, so very nigh to God;
I cannot nearer be;
For in the person of His Son
I am as near as He.

So dear, so very dear to God;
Dearer I cannot be -
The love wherewith He loves His Son,
Such is His love to me.

Why should I ever careful be
Since such a God is mine;
He watches o'er me night and day,
And tells me, 'Mine is thine.'

Willie seemed to enjoy it, and said, 'Papa, will you sing that at my funeral?'

'Yes, dear, if you want it.'

'Yes, I would like it very much.'

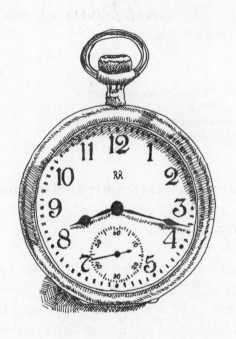

Last Days

'Beguiling waiting hours
With rapturous thoughts of Home;
Breathing a yearning whisper –
"When will the Master come?"'

His father and I went down to breakfast, leaving Uncle Joseph beside him.

'What day is this, Uncle?'

'Saturday.'

'You should go down for your dinner, too.'

'It's only breakfast time yet.'

'Then I'll have a chance to get away today yet. I hope Jesus will not be displeased at me for being so impatient to get away, but I'm wearying to be home. I thought I would not have seen another day.'

Joseph said, 'I'm not disappointed, Willie, that you have.'

'But I'm very disappointed!'

He asked us to engage in prayer in turn before he parted with Uncle Joseph. His Uncle David had come, and was present also. I knelt close to Willie, and had his hand in mine. He said, with a smile, 'Mother, will do it first.'

I shook my head, and said quietly, 'No, Willie, the others will pray. You know I don't like, before others.'

He just smiled sweetly again, squeezed my hand, and said, 'You first, mother.'

Uncle Joseph left, undecided whether to return on Saturday evening, or to join his little family at Luss, and return on Monday. Willie could not help him to decide. He wanted him, oh so much! But then his wee boys, and Aunt Maggie also, must be wanting him.

'Underneath are the everlasting arms' seemed often to become just a couch for him to lie down on.

'Do you want to send any message to Hendry or Willie? You were too ill to see them when they called.'

'Let them follow Jesus; but I think they are doing that.'

'Mother, will you hold one hand, and Papa the other, at the very end?'

Several times on Saturday he looked to us and said, 'Now, a hand each!' thinking that it was the end.

Speaking to his sisters and Cousin Jeanie, at his side, he all at once said, in a quiet, easy way, 'Agnes, dear, if you are not long of coming after me, and want to leave a little thing to each of the others, as I am doing, get textbooks, I advise you. They can carry them in their pockets always, and read a verse as they need. I wish I had one for my pocket.'

He began to think and speak a great deal about 'the Water of Life.' It seemed to be a very sweet, soothing thought to him. He felt great weariedness and tiredness, and the thought of 'the Water of Life' seemed to refresh his weary spirit.

I said, 'My poor darling, you are very tired.'

'Very, very tired, mother dear.'

'Oh, but you are going to get a sweet rest soon, in that lovely home!'

'Oh, yes, Mother; when I get there I'll just lie down on the bank of the river for a rest, and take such a big drink of the water, clear as crystal!'

I quoted these two texts to him: 'There remaineth therefore a rest,'and, 'They rest not day nor night,' adding, 'I think that last "rest" will be the one you will like best!'

He smiled sweetly at this reference to his old restless activity, which had been so often a trouble to us, and said, 'Oh, I'll be glad, glad to get the first "rest" first, and then the second!'

'How nice it will be, Willie, to see all the loved folk yonder, with Jesus in their midst! What a welcome and what a kiss Regie will give you, his old 'Crosshill boy'!'

He smiled and answered, 'Yes, the dear wee boy!' In a few moments he added, 'I wonder if Jesus will let me kiss Him!…perhaps His feet… with the marks!'

He wrote on Agnes' Bible the text, 'He asked life of Thee, and Thou gavest him length of days for ever and ever' (Psalm 21: 4). He had scarcely to finish. He gave it to her and kissed her, saying, 'Papa will explain to you what I have written.'

When Agnes had gone, he said, 'Papa, or Mother, will you explain the verse I have written on her Bible?' Years ago, his father and I had talked over this verse with him in a churchyard in Eskdalemuir.

'Mother, wouldn't it be nice to get George (grandmamma's coachman for about ten years) to drive me?… You could easily get him if you get the things from Wylie and Lochhead. He is now in their employ, you know. Wouldn't you like it?' (To drive his body to the grave, he meant.)

Immediately after his Uncle Joseph had left, he had a time of ease; and was lying looking out on the bright, fresh morning, with a pleasant, restful expression on his face.

'I would like to get a drive in Uncle Joseph's phaeton! It would be so nice to get a breath of fresh air! What say you, mother?'

'Willie, could you stand the fatigue of moving?'

'Maybe; what do you think?'

I was quite perplexed, not knowing what to make of this request. I could scarcely take in that he was really in earnest. 'I don't know – I never thought of such a thing; but if you think you could bear to be moved at all, we'll take you out in a chair at once.'

'Oh, no, dear mother; I wouldn't like that at all. Just the thought that it was dear Uncle Joseph's phaeton might have strengthened me.'

I had recovered myself then, and saw it was just a fancy, and could not be thought of for a moment. So I said cheerily to him, 'Oh, my boy, you'll get fine fresh air soon, and golden chariots too, to drive in! Just a little more patience, and you'll have all you want.'

He asked me to take him in my arms, that he might lean his head on me. I sang very softly to him, and he seemed to have fallen into a sweet, quiet sleep. I was sitting perfectly still, with him in my arms, when I was startled with a strange, sweet, glad, surprised look coming over his face, although he did not open his eyes. Then the words came very brightly, but slowly, 'Oh, there they are! They're coming! Oh, how lovely!'

'What is it, dear?' I whispered.

'Chariots! Golden chariots! A great many! But they are passing the foot of the road! They're not coming for me!' The tone was a little disappointed, so I whispered again, 'Oh, yes, they'll come soon for you.'

'Oh, what a great company!'

'What is it like?' I said.

'Oh, a great company of people gathered! Oh, what a lot of chariots! They are passing, though. They are not coming this way!'

Then in a grieved tone he said, in a few minutes, moving his head uneasily on my breast, 'Mother, Satan is teasing me!'

'How, dear?'

'He's showing me lots of nice things, and not letting me get them!'

'Oh, never mind, darling; the nice things are not Satan's. He can neither give them to you, nor keep them from you. Jesus will give you all at the right time. Just a little more waiting!'

'Oh, that's good!' he said, with a sigh of relief.

I was sent to rest for a little, and as grandmamma and Father were with Willie, I very quickly fell asleep. After some hours I was wakened with a soft kiss on my cheek. It was my mother. She said, 'Oh, I am sorry to waken you; but he wants you very much.'

I learnt from her that she had insisted upon Willie's father lying down on the couch beside Willie, and that he too was sleeping. I went at once to him. He threw his arms round my neck, and burst into tears.

'Oh, Mother! You and Papa should not both have left me. Satan has been teasing me awfully! You must not leave me again. When you are beside me ready to say one of God's holy words, it stays my mind, and Satan does not get near.'

He was trembling and greatly agitated, and unnerved. Taking him by the hand, I first of all asked him if he had forgotten that His ear was ever open to his cry, and that though father and mother were sleeping, Jesus never slept? I assured him that Jesus saw it all, and asked if he remembered who said, 'I have prayed for thee, that thy faith fail not'; 'None is able to pluck them out of My Father's hand,'? He was calmed at once by two or three such promises, but asked me to keep on saying verses for a while, 'in case Satan should again begin to trouble him.' I pointed to his father, still quietly sleeping almost within touch of Willie, and said, 'Ah, Willie, why did you not wake Papa?'

He looked at him through his tears, and said, 'He looked so wearied, I couldn't think to do it.'

He thought I was leaving the room again, when I rose to get a Bible which was lying on the table, so I said, to set his mind at rest, 'No, darling; I'll not leave you again till you are safe with Jesus.'

'Oh, thank you, Mother! I hope it'll not be long.'

I read on verse after verse in the Psalms (after a word of prayer with him). He had hold of my one hand firmly, and if I paused for a minute, he squeezed my hand to go on. As I had not time to choose passages, and had only one hand to turn the leaves, I just cried in my heart to the Lord to quicken my eyesight and direct verses which He would make 'Spirit and Life' to dear Willie. I observed that he felt these verses to be very precious, by the earnest moving of his lips and the audible 'Amen!' every now and again.

By and by I sang the Psalm, 'Jehovah hear thee in the day when trouble He doth send,' and that hymn, 'One is kind above all others.' He soon got quite over this, and became bright and happy again.

'Mother, I want you never to give James intoxicating drink, even as a medicine. I have spoken to him about this, and I don't think he'll ever touch it.'

When alone with his father and grandmamma, the latter said to him, 'Willie, isn't it nice to think that even at the eleventh hour Jesus will welcome and save, as He did the thief on the cross?'

Willie turned to her and said, 'Grandmamma, I'm very glad I did not leave it to the eleventh hour. If I had, I could not have come to Jesus at all; I have been so distressed with this pain. Oh, dear gran'ma, I hope you'll get easier through; I hope you'll not have to suffer so much pain!'

Speaking once more of the great kindness and considerate attention he had received from friends and neighbours, he said, 'Do not forget to thank them all. You might call on them after, and thank them, Mother. Everybody has been so kind, I don't know what to say.'

We were led on to speak of Livingstone, and of the lonely circumstances in which he died.

But we need not go so far as Livingstone. Think of that man who worked in the mill; did Uncle Joseph tell you about him?'

'No, dear.'

'Oh, Mother, just think of it! In Glasgow! When uncle went to ask for him, he had to get the key of is door from a neighbour downstairs! He lives with his mother, and she has to go out and work. Uncle says he is dying! Dying so lonely, in the midst of so many! I think that's even worse than Livingstone!'

When moving him a little in the bed, he seemed to feel his inability to help me, and smilingly said, 'Just a clod of the valley now, Mother!'

Then a thought seemed to strike him, and he said, 'I doubt you'll have a bother 'after'! . . . But,' as if he had come to a solution of the difficulty, 'get Papa to help you, dear mother!'

He had some quiet, peaceful times on Saturday; but as the afternoon wore on, he grew more distressed. I noticed that when he fell into a short sleep, his left hand always moved up to one spot on his chest, and settled there till he woke up. I asked him if his chest was not all sore. He looked up into my face calmly and without a shadow of fretfulness, and said, 'All sore, mother dear; but this spot . . . terrible pain, te-rr-ible pain!'

I sang at this time the hymn which had been his favourite from the beginning, and which he had said he would like sung at the end — McCheyne's 'Jehovah Tsidkenu.'

After singing the last verse, Willie said, looking earnestly to me, 'Oh, this has been an awful fever, Mother!'

'Yes, my dear; but God will set you free soon.'

'Oh, Mother, I wish Jesus would come for me!'

'Well, dear, He is coming.'

'Oh, but I wish He would come soon.'

'Well, I'll be glad to know that you are away safe with Him; but you'll try and be patient, and wait His will. You told me that you would like to glorify God here, because He was taking you so soon and so quickly to enjoy Him for ever.'

'But, Mother, I'm not glorifying Him!'

'Yes, my boy, you are.'

'How?'

'By the way you have borne this illness all through.'

'Oh, I'm so glad! I didn't know I had been patient.'

'Indeed, you have been very patient, Willie, and very thoughtful of others; everybody, even your doctors, wonder at it!' We had never said a word of this kind to him hitherto, and I believe I was led to speak this sustaining word at the moment when heart and flesh were fainting and failing.

'I am very thankful for that, Mother,' he said, with great earnestness. In a few minutes after, he said, 'Perhaps, I shouldn't be told that.'

'Why, dear?'

'Just because it might make me feel I've been a very good boy!' (with a smile).

'My darling there's hardly room for that. You know very well that quick, restless, impatient Willie Riddell could never have lain there with that leg, without a murmur, if it had not been for Jesus; and neither could I sit by your side these days if it were not for Jesus.'

'I see that, and know it too . . . but . . . perhaps I had better not hear anything of that kind again; Satan might use it. Papa, you might pray; ask Him to come now for me.'

His father hesitated. I said, 'Willie, you want to glorify Him; now in asking Jesus to come just now for you, you do not know what you are asking. Wouldn't it be better to leave the time entirely to Him? He knows best.'

'Oh, yes, you're right; I was just impatient. Ask Him to come soon, not to let it be very long.'

Anticipations of the End

'I shall wander at His side
Where the living waters glide;
And these feet shall need no guard
On the unbroken heavenly sward.

* * * *

'Hark! He turns the admitting key,
Smiles in love, and welcomes me.'

From six to seven he suffered great uneasiness, and did not seem able to get rest in any way. A little before seven, he said, in a decided tone, 'Mother, I think I'll try to sleep, if you'll make me comfortable.'

He gave me very explicit directions about laying him right and straight in the middle of the bed, and making his bed perfectly neat and tidy. He then gave me an affectionate kiss, and said solemnly, 'Goodnight, dear mother; come and sit by me. I feel a little cold.'

I pressed the clothes in at his back. He smiled and said, 'You know I can't bear to be bound.' I had to free them again. I offered to get a hot bottle.

'No; I don't want it, mother; I'm all right. Come and sit beside me.'

I though his manner strange at the time; and afterwards, when looking back, I could not but think that Dear Willie had 'gathered up' himself to die. As I passed round to my seat, I heard him say very softly and solemnly, —

> 'And now I lay me down to sleep,
> I give myself to Christ to keep;
> If I should die before I wake,
> I pray thee, Saviour, my soul take.'

'Mother, I think we have been wrong; I have always been getting someone to pray for me. I think Jesus would rather that I should do it myself; but I have been so ill and distressed, that I was glad to have you all do it for me. I think I must try and do it myself after this.'

I reminded him that a word or even a thought directed to Jesus was enough, that His eye was ever resting on him, that all through this illness, He had seen and known about every pang; and that our God waits that He may be gracious. I then offered him his medicine — chloric ether — but he refused it, saying, 'No, Mother dear; I think I would like to get a sleep without any medicine tonight.'

'Oh, I think you had better take your mixture, dear.'

'Oh, no; I would like a sleep straight from Jesus tonight.'

'Very well, darling; that'll be a much sweeter sleep.'

Instead of putting his hand into mine, as usual, I noted that he put it under his cheek, as he always did in days of health. Grandmamma was sitting near, Father was on the couch at the other end of the room. Willie seemed to have fallen asleep. By-and-by I noticed the lips moving; then I heard him whisper for a minute or two, then the voice gradually became distinct, although very peculiar and far-away-like: 'I am very tired; take me to Thyself. I have been wearying for Thee, Lord..., and bless dear father and mother. Comfort them when I am away; and restore their health and strength, that they may do Thy work here; and help them to care for all these little ones, and teach them about Thee. Help them to

119

bring them all to Thee... Tomorrow is my first communion with Thee, Jesus.'

I rose to touch my husband that he might come and hear also, so that I must have missed some words. What we heard next was, 'I think I'll row up the stream and meet Him.' Then his head kept moving as if he were tiredly rowing, with labouring breath.

'I am a little weary: I cannot row any further, Jesus. I'll just anchor here and wait till you come . . . I have just on my old clothes, but you'll put your cloak on me — for it is cold out here — and warm me, Jesus, before I sit down at Thy supper... This is the way! I see the way now... I have lost the way again... Oh, there's One that seems to know the way; I'll follow Him. His boat is bigger than mine... Oh, there's the harbour now! I don't see it again! You can steer best now, Jesus! Steer me! I'll let you steer, Jesus! I thought you did not see me coming! ... Oh, I am so tired. Let me hold on to you, Jesus, till I am recovered again. Take me home. Let me get warmed, and it'll go away ... Yes ... Don't speak to me! His father had whispered a word to me. Let me go with Him. A little sore? What's that scratching noise? Are we scratching the bottom yet? ... Yonder's the place! ... The day is breaking! It's early here! Come soon! ... I think

I'll come in just now, and leave my present down there. You can send for it again ... It's nice and warm! Oh, this is nice!'

The laboured rowing seemed then to cease, and he gave a deep sigh, and wakened up shortly after, speaking as if to himself more than to us, 'I don't know how I missed Him! I should just have waited, but I was very cold waiting, and I thought I would try to meet Him; but I am not going to try any more. I'm only going to wait; perhaps they hadn't it quite prepared.'

His uncle, seeing him breathing with such difficulty, said, 'He saw thee toiling in rowing.'

'I wonder if He saw me!'

'Yes, He saw you.'

'Well, I wonder why He did not come to me! Perhaps He wasn't pleased at my going to meet Him when He told me to wait.'

His father said, 'Isn't it nice to think that you and Jesus will soon meet? You are wearying for Him, and that just tells us that He is wearying for you.'

'Does it? It didn't look like it these two times;' referring to the passing of the chariots and the rowing.

They all came to say goodnight. They were deeply grieved to see him so ill. John bent his head on the bed and wept. Willie patted his head lovingly, and said, 'Come, John, no crying allowed here.'

When John turned to go, I said, 'Dear John, follow Willie.'

'Oh, no! Don't follow me!' Willie urged turning to me. 'He may go far wrong if he follows me.' Then, as John had passed out of his sight, he raised his voice and called after him, 'Follow Jesus, John!'

When in great distress from the pain in his chest, he turned with a very anxious expression of face to me, saying, 'Oh, don't let the children come just now.'

As the house was quite still at the time, I could not understand him, but just said in answer, 'No, dear, I'll not.' He still looked at me, and made a sign to me to go, saying, 'Oh, keep them from coming; they would be so vexed to see me this way.'

'They are not coming, Willie; they can't come' (all were sleeping).

He turned to his father, as if he thought I must be mistaken, and looked to him to confirm this, when I said, 'There's nobody here but father, mother – and Jesus – He's come!'

The anxious expression passed from his face in an instant, and he lay back on his pillows with a sweet, restful smile, saying, 'Oh, it would be He. That's nice, that's nice.'

We thought, 'How sweet the Name of Jesus sounds,' etc.

He often asked, 'What o'clock is it?' and seemed to be 'wearying for Christ to come' for him.

One time when his father answered him what hour it was, he looked very disappointed (he always appeared as if he expected it to be a few hours further on), then said, 'Well, I'll ask no more about time; I'll just wait for eternity.'

He asked his father to do something to his leg; in a little while, again he asked him to do the same, but added, 'Oh, never mind, Papa; don't trouble – it's not worth while. I really don't care much how my legs are now, if Jesus is coming tonight.'

He felt a little hungry, and Cathie made him some gruel, which he seemed to relish (taken through an India –rubber tube, as it hurt him to raise him, and he did not like a drinking cup. The tube was his own idea).

'Uncle David, do you remember our last sail up the Kyles in the Ariel, when you turned ill, and we had to manage the boat?'

His father said, 'That would be splendid, Willie.'

'Oh, it was splendid; but not when the poor captain's white face looked up from the cabin.'

We raised him and arranged his pillow.

'What an idea, that I must be lifted about in this way!'

David said, 'I am afraid you wouldn't be of much use in the Ariel now.'

'No; I would just be in the way. You might sing to me. I can't think on Jesus when I am in pain. Will He be angry?'

'No, no. He knows how pained you are.'

'Well, I would like to think of Him, and if you sing, it will help me.'

His father began a hymn.

'No, no, father, sing a psalm. Sing the 23rd Psalm, or the 63rd, or the 103rd. The Psalms fit.'

We sang the 23rd, and at the third verse – 'Yea, though I walk in death's dark vale,' etc., he sang along with us clearly. As we finished, he said, 'That's nice. I'm thirsty; soon I'll drink of the Water of Life. Papa, I would like a greengage.'

His father was proceeding to peal one; Willie said, 'Oh, don't peal it, please. You know I like the skin, Papa; and it can't do me any harm now, if Jesus is coming tonight.'

After eating his greengage, he said, 'What made you think, Mother, that Jesus would come for me tonight?' (I had not said anything about this, but did not disclaim it, in case of discouraging him.)

'Oh, the 'tokens' you told us about.'

'Oh, yes; I forgot. I hope He'll come tonight; but that's looking ahead again. Now, Papa, we promised to say nothing about time, only about eternity. You know I thought I would see Jesus last night; but I am going to wait tonight, and tomorrow night, and the next night, if He likes.'

His father said, 'You'll thank Him for me that He has been so good to you.'

Uncle David said, 'He has been so good to you, we all feel thankful. You will have to thank Him for all us all.'

'Yes, if I can; but I have so much of my own to thank Him for; plenty to take up all my time, without yours.'

He fell asleep about eleven, and at twelve o'clock he awoke. His father and I were alone. Turning such a look of love first on the one and then on the other, he kissed us and fondled us, as if we had been long parted, and then said, 'Dear father, dear mother, I am so happy, — oh – I – am – so – happy! and well! This is quite comfortable. I wish Uncle Joseph had come; I feel so well and happy. Isn't it kind of Jesus giving me such a peaceful, happy time before I go? I wonder if John is sleeping? Don't waken him if he is; but I would like to speak to him.'

When John was brought from his room, Willie turned over on his left side for the first time since he had been ill, and took the poor sorrow—stricken boy into his arms.

'John, you dear boy, come in here beside me.'

John hesitated.

'You are not afraid of me, are you, John?'

'No, but I am afraid of hurting your leg.'

'Oh, John, my leg has no pain in it now; don't be frightened. I am all well now.'

John got in beside him, and Willie fondled and petted him for a little, trying to comfort him, then said, 'John, I wanted you to come and see for yourself that death is not what you and I used to think it. We were all wrong about death. We don't die at all. Jesus died. But this is how it is. This body of mine has been going on for seventeen and a half years, and it is tired, very tired, and it must be laid in the grave for a long rest; but my spirit is not the least tired, and it will go straight to Jesus. Then you know, there, a thousand years are like one day; so I'll not be weary. I'll only have time to do one or two messages for Jesus till you come, and then it'll just be "John and Willie" again, as it used to be; and you know, dear John, it can't be a thousand years for you at any rate – perhaps not very long at all; so you can't weary much either.' Then, looking up to me, he said, 'Now remember, Mother, it's not "dying", and not "death," but just, — "And they who live shall changed be."'

We sang the whole of McCheyne's hymn, 'Jehovah Tsidkenu.'

'I once was a stranger to grace and to God,
I knew not my danger and felt not my load;
Though friends spoke in rapture of Christ on the tree,
Jehovah Tsidkenu was nothing to me.

'Like tears from the daughters of Zion that roll,
I wept when the waters went over His soul;
Yet thought not that my sins had nailed to the tree
Jehovah Tsidkenu – 'twas nothing to me.

'When free grace awoke me, by light from on high,
Then legal fears shook me, I trembled to die;
No refuge, no safety, in self could I see, —
Jehovah Tsidkenu my Saviour must be.

'My terrors all vanished before the sweet name;
My guilty fears vanished, with boldness I came
To drink at the fountain, life—giving and free, —
Jehovah Tsidkenu is all things to me.

'Even treading the valley, the shadow of death,
This watchword shall rally my faltering breath;
For when from life's fever my God sets me free,
Jehovah Tsidkenu my death-song shall be.'

He sang tenor quite correctly, with John still lying in his arms. As we finished the last verse.

'Jehovah Tsidkenu my death-song shall be;'

'"Life-song" it should be, Papa, not "death-song!"'

The four eldest had always sung to me in the evenings after lessons, and this had been a great pleasure. He often expressed regret that his father had to be out night after night. I said, after the hymn had been sung, 'What am I to do now without my quartette?' Willie looked up in his father's face, half—shyly, half—roguishly, 'Take Papa in, instead of me. How nice this is! Oh, it's very good of Him to give me this little while! Although I had lived ever so long, I would never have forgotten this time. The Lord has been very good and kind to me! Now, Mother, you and Papa must just love and serve Him better than ever for all His kindness to me. I can't tell you all He has done for me. The way He has heard and answered my prayers, about things that you know, and about things that you don't know; it's just wonderful!'

Fully an hour and a half was thus spent in a way that can never be forgotten. The oppression in his chest returned. He sent his brother back to his own room again. His suffering became very hard to bear, and he longed for 'His coming.' We did what we could to 'stay' his mind. We reminded him that the death of His saints was a precious thing to the Lord; that the Saviour's eye was now resting on his death-bed; that underneath were the everlasting arms. We spoke to him about Stephen's death, reminded him of how when Stephen was suffering such terrible pain from the cruel stoning, God had graciously drawn aside the veil and given him a glimpse of what was just before him — Jesus, the Son of Man — standing ready to receive his spirit at the right time. Dear Willie was deeply interested in all that we said. A little while after we noticed him looking inquiringly up and down and around, then he said, 'But I don't see Him, Papa.'

'Ah, but He sees you,' I said. 'You'll not see Him and us at the same time, but when you stop seeing us, you'll see Him.'

'Oh, is that the way? Oh, that will be so nice!'

Crossing the River

'Not one billow shall go o'er thee
I am on the way before thee.'

On Sabbath morning, at 6 a.m., his father went to bed, and his Uncle David came beside Willie. He was lying with his eyes closed, when he suddenly said, in a bright, eager way, 'I think I see Him coming now! Yes! The thing I have long looked for is come at last! It's growing bright now!'

Thinking from his look that he might be right, I said to his uncle, 'Get Papa.' He opened his eyes then, and said, 'No, don't waken Papa, for perhaps I'll be cheated this time too. Make the window dark.'

His uncle let down one blind — 'darker' — he let down another.

'Very dark,' he said anxiously. Then came a sore struggle. He seemed as if being suffocated. His uncle said something about a river, and

Willie seemed as if he realized himself getting beyond his depth. I said in my dismay, 'Oh, Willie, there's no river.' He put up his hand toward me, as if to correct me, saying, 'Yes, Mother, there is a river, and this is it;' but added, 'but it's just a step more.'

I was quite overcome, the attack had come on so suddenly. When I was able to lift my head again, I met his sympathising, sorrowful look; and he held out his hand to me to take, saying, with great tenderness, 'My dear mother! O Lord Jesus, come quickly!'

I looked to Uncle David to get my husband. When he went, Willie turned to me earnestly, saying, 'Oh, Mother, can you and Uncle David not think of something to save from this earthly drowning? Oh, it's hard dying for want of breath! Why does He not come quickly?'

I said, 'He has some good reason for keeping you here, for your good or for ours.'

'Oh, yes; I will trust Him, but it's hard waiting for Christ in this way! Pray, uncle, [who had now returned] that He may come quickly!' He joined most earnestly in the petitions presented; then after the 'amen,' he said, 'Oh, how nice it would be now just to be taken gently in His arms!'

He was threatened with a cough, and, with a distressed, frightened look, he said, 'Oh, I'll burst if I cough again; I'm sure I'll burst!'

'Well, then, Willie, your spirit will get free.'

'Will it?' He asked as if he had forgotten. 'Oh, then it's all right.'

His father said, 'Yes, "Though I walk through the valley of the shadow of death, I will fear no evil; for Thou art with me."'

Willie said, 'Oh, there's no evil from Him, the dear, loving Lord.'

His father said, 'Jehovah-Rophi.'

Willie responded: 'He has healed me.'

This sore attack was the worst he had to suffer. WE never saw a look of pain, nor even of anxiety on the loved countenance again. We gave him his medicine rather oftener.

When his uncle was leaving for church (he was to preach for Mr. Riddell), he said to Willie, 'Would you like the congregation to pray for you?'

'Yes, uncle; tell them to pray that I may get patience, and that Jesus may come for me soon.'

'John, you are not going to church? Oh, no, you mustn't; I want you.'

Uncle James said, 'Willie, what about so many staying at home from church?'

'Oh, uncle, I think for one day it's quite allowable. I don't want James to be away!'

When I offered him his mixture, he said, 'Mother, do you think it is right to take it so often?'

'Yes, if it eases you.'

'Oh, yes, it does; but do you think it is right, when Jesus sends this pain?'

'Yes, dear; I am quite sure it is. Jesus made these opiates, and taught men how to use them for the lessening of pain in this poor suffering world.'

'Very well, just give me it.' In a while after, his father came into the room and sat beside him. He turned eagerly to him, saying, 'Oh, never be afraid to give these medicines to anybody ill like this!' He noticed that the bottled had been newly filled, and the next time I gave him some, he looked anxiously after it, as I laid it down on a side-table, and said, 'Mother, dear, take care where you set that medicine. That's not a thing any one should touch that does not need it.'

He was now very weak, and lay quiet most of the day. Grandmamma, Uncle James, John, Father, and I were with him while the rest were at church. It was a solemn day of waiting for the coming of the Bridegroom! Once, when we were all sitting with bowed heads, with no sound but that of Willie's hard breathing, his father lifted his face from his hands, and said, 'And sitting down they watched him there.' The words brought vividly up before us that great redemption work – accomplished for us – through which we were now able to sit down and watch calmly and trustfully, although so sorrowfully.

About 3 p.m. he awoke from a short sleep, and after I had wiped the sweat from his face and hands, he said so pleasantly, 'Mother, could you read about "the tokens"* now? Papa has not got doing it yet to John and Grandmamma.'

'Yes, if you wish it, and if it would not tire you too much to hear it.'

'Oh, I would like it now.'

I gave the book to Uncle James and Willie gave me his hand to hold, saying, 'Now, grandmamma and John, listen!'

When James came to the 'tokens,' he said, looking over to gran'ma, 'Grandmamma, you have got two of these already.'

I said, 'What are they?'

'Oh, you know, Mother, — the turn she had once here, and one she had in her own house.'

The continued sound of reading tried him very much; but he was so eager that grandmamma

135

and John should hear, that he would not listen to our proposals to give him rest.

Once when James stopped that he might get a drink of water, and have the sweat dried and his pillow changed, he said quite cheerily when it was all done: 'Now, ladies and gentlemen, I am ready!'

While James was reading, he squeezed my hand to attract my attention, and said in a low tone, 'Mother, do you see any 'tokens' on my face?'

I looked, but said nothing.

'Tell me, Mother. I asked John, but I think he didn't like to tell me; he was vexed.'

'Well, I see tokens enough on your face, that tell me you'll soon be yonder seeing the "King in His beauty."'

'Besides the medicine ones; are you sure?'

'Oh, yes.'

'Oh, I am very glad!' And he lay back on his pillow with a satisfied look. As he was getting very weak, and for a while unconscious, we thought he might be away before they returned from church. When they got home, he was pleased to see them. Uncle told him a bit of the sermon, and that they had prayed for him.

All left to go down to tea, and immediately Willie said, in a strangely altered voice: 'Is father here? Mother, is Papa in the room?'

'No, darling; he has just gone down to tea. Shall I call him, or can you wait? He is very tired, dear, and would be better if you could let him have ten minutes to get something to eat. '

'Oh, yes, dear father! Mother, when they come up from tea, will you divide my fruit amongst them. I want them all to get some.'

About half past six they all gathered into his room again. I told them his wish, and his Uncle James did as he desired. Willie said: 'Papa, if you come across a nice yellow gooseberry, put it into my mouth.'

His father did so, and Willie said smilingly,

'Now I have got my share of the feast.'

Uncle James said, 'This is like a love-feast before the parting, Willie!'

'Yes, isn't it nice, uncle?'

He asked for a drink of water. 'I want it from John; where is he? Now will you raise me up? I don't want it through the tube.'

John brought it.

'Now thank you, John,' and he took the tumbler in his own hands, his uncles supporting him in their arms. He took a big drink, then they laid him gently back on his pillows, and he said, 'Oh, that's splendid! That's splendid! I never got anything so nice! Tell John [who had gone out of sight with the tumbler] it is the nicest thing I have got for many a day! There's no drink like God's drink.'

He did this again almost every halfhour, asking it from John, and asking to be raised.

His father said to his cousin: 'Jeanie, your gooseberries are the last thing Willie enjoyed.'

'No, Papa; I had something since – a drink of real water from John. I wouldn't have missed that for anything.'

His sisters and cousin were leaving for the night.

'Have you anything to say to the girls, dear? Will you tell them to follow Jesus?'

'Oh, yes; they'll learn all about it in the Bible and in their textbooks.'

All went away to their rooms about half past ten, leaving his father, James, and me with the weary boy. He spoke little after this. He never omitted to say, 'Thank you,' after each little attention.

As midnight approached, he grew very weak. His father knelt at his side, speaking precious words of life into his ear till the very end. I was lying on a couch at the other end of the room, and as the words of God fell on my ear, 'Apples of gold in pictures of silver' seemed but a poor description of their beauty and fitness to the needs of that trying hour. James was lying on a sofa nearer Willie. At twenty minutes from twelve, his father offered him a little of his medicine, which he declined. He then gave him one more drink of water, and we heard distinctly the faint, 'Thank you.' He laid down the tumbler, and turning to Willie, he said, as he smoothed back his hair, 'My own boy... Jesus' own boy!' It was sweet to hear the echo from his dying lips, 'Yes, Jesus' own boy!'

We rose and came to his side. He gave one long sigh, and his eyes, opening widely, filled with a strange, unearthly brightness. In a second or two this was repeated, and our darling's spirit was free.

> *'Shielded and safe from sorrow;*
> *At home at last,'*

at ten minutes from twelve, Sabbath night, 5th August, 1883.

'Sleep on, beloved, sleep and take thy rest,
Lay down thy head upon thy Saviour's breast;
We love thee well, but Jesus loves thee best, —
                                Good—night.

'Calm is thy slumber as an infant's sleep,
But thou shalt wake no more to toil and weep.
Thine is a perfect rest, secure and deep, —
                                Good—night.

'Until the shadow from this earth is cast,
Until He gathers in His sheaves at last,
Until the twilight gloom is overpast, —
                                Good—night.

'Until the Easter glory light the skies,
Until the dead in Jesus shall arise,
And He shall come, but not in lowly guise, —
                                Good—night.

'Until, made beautiful by love divine,
Thou in the likeness of thy Lord shalt shine,
And He shall bring that golden crown of thine, —
                                Good—night.

'Only 'Good—night,' beloved - not farewell!
'A little while,' and all His saints shall dwell
In   hallowed   union   indivisible,   —
                                Good—night.

'Until we meet again before His throne,
Clothed in the spotless robes He gives His own,
Until we know even as we are known, —
                                Good—night.

Dear Willie was buried beside his grandpapa and little brother, on the 8th of August. Three months after, the grave had to be opened again, to let the body of the 'sweet little Edith May' rest by his side.

'Joy cometh in the morning,' when 'they that are in their graves shall hear the voice of the Son of Man, and shall come forth.'

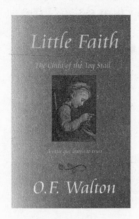

Little Faith
A little girl learns to trust
O.F. Walton

Faith, persecuted by her grandmother when her mother dies, finds faith and justice.

ISBN: 1 85792 567X

Christie's Old Organ
A little boy's journey to find a home of his own
O.F. Walton

Christie is a street child. He sets out with Treffy, the Organ Grinder, to find a place of peace.

ISBN: 1 85792 5238

Classic Fiction Titles

A Peep Behind the Scenes
A little girl's journey of discovery

O.F. Walton

Rosalie is forced from place to place with her brutal father's travelling theatre - if only she could find a real loving relationship?

ISBN: 1 85792 5246

A Basket of Flowers
A young girls fight against injustice

Christoph von Schmid

Falsely accused of theft, thrown from her home, her father dead - Mary learns to trust God.
Exciting tale with a dramatic twist.

ISBN: 1 85792 5254

CHRISTIAN FOCUS

Staying Faithful - Reaching Out!

Christian Focus Publications publishes books for adults and children under its three main imprints: Christian Focus, Mentor and Christian Heritage. Our books reflect that God's word is reliable and Jesus is the way to know him, and live for ever with him.

Our children's publication list includes a Sunday school curriculum that covers pre-school to early teens; puzzle and activity books. We also publish personal and family devotional titles, biographies and inspirational stories that children will love.

If you are looking for quality Bible teaching for children then we have an excellent range of Bible story and age specific theological books.

From pre-school to teenage fiction, we have it covered!

Find us at our web page:
www.christianfocus.com